Penguin Books

Neglected Lives

Stephen Alter is an American who was born and raised in India, where his parents worked as missionaries. He completed his education at Wesleyan University, Connecticut. He has made a special study of the history of the British in India, where both his novels take place. *Neglected Lives*, which is Stephen Alter's first novel, has received widespread praise. His second novel, *Silk and Steel* (1980), is set close to Mussoorie, Uttar Pradesh, where he lives.

Stephen Alter

Neglected Lives

Penguin Books

Penguin Books Ltd, Harmondsworth, Middlesex, England
Penguin Books, 625 Madison Avenue, New York, New York 10022, U.S.A.
Penguin Books Australia Ltd, Ringwood, Victoria, Australia
Penguin Books Canada Ltd, 2801 John Street, Markham, Ontario, Canada L3R 1B4
Penguin Books (N.Z.) Ltd, 182–190 Wairau Road, Auckland 10, New Zealand

First published in the U.S.A. by Farrar Straus Giroux, New York 1978
First published in Great Britain by André Deutsch Ltd 1979
Published in Penguin Books 1982

Made and printed in Great Britain by
Richard Clay (The Chaucer Press) Ltd, Bungay, Suffolk
Set in Plantin

For my parents
Robert and Ellen Alter

The place, the people,
and the incidents in this book
are all fictional

Contents

Neglected Lives

ONE . *Fascination*

My dear Lionel,

Take the train from Lucknow to Jamshedpur. From there the best way to get to Kanjiwalla, which is at the foot of the hill, is by tonga. It's about half an hour's trip if the horse is fast. Most of the drivers are young and will crowd around you at the station gate. Don't ride with any of them. Their horses are underfed and slow. Ask for Bhola Ram. It is likely they will say he has gone to Jhabra for his niece's wedding or to Rambad for his cousin's nephew's, which won't be true. Bhola Ram probably doesn't have a niece or a cousin with a nephew. His tonga is always parked under the big neem tree by the post office. He will be asleep. His turban will have slid to one side; he will be snoring, and his white whiskers will be tied in a knot under his chin. The younger men will try to persuade you that he is not well and not taking riders today. Don't listen to them. Wake him up and tell him that you are a guest of Augden Sahib's and would like him to take you to Kanjiwalla. That is enough. He will load your luggage onto the back, help you into your seat, yell at the other drivers, and then with a word – the younger men use a switch – he will set his horse at a gallop up the road. His horse is well fed and wins the Jamshedpur races every year.

At Kanjiwalla, Bhola Ram will arrange everything for you. Whether you want a horse or a dandie, he will get you the best price. He will refuse to take anything for himself. Give him a rupee anyway. Eventually he will accept it and salute.

The ride up to Debrakot takes about three hours. Most of it is unpleasant. The road is badly cut and washed away in spots. If you decide to take a horse, the saddle will probably be broken and pinch you. The dandie is a more comfortable ride, but only if the men know how to carry it properly. They are supposed to walk out of step to avoid jogging you. Nowadays, though, among other things, they are forgetting how to carry dandies. They have no consideration for the rider any more, and probably wouldn't give a damn if you bounced out. A few of the older coolies remember and if they think you've been around they'll give you a good ride. Talk to them in Hindi, if you have the patience. They like that and will try to make you as comfortable as possible.

I'll meet you at the 'havagarh'. That's about three quarters of the way up. I don't like to take the horses down any farther when it's hot weather like this. They're hill ponies and get sick in the heat.

You were born in Debrakot. I remember, your mother came up and stayed with us. There was a civil hospital here then. Now we all go to Dr Pande. He's retired but he keeps an office in his house. You wouldn't remember Debrakot. You were too small. Even if you could, you wouldn't recognize it now. The town has changed completely.

I'm glad your father felt free to write to me, Lionel. Since a long time back I've been trying to get him to come up for a visit. Perhaps he will, now that you're here. I remember you only as a toddler. We were in Lucknow for a month in 1955. That's when I last saw you. We came and stayed with your parents. All you did was cry and pee the whole time. We were worried that you'd get dehydrated. This is the sort of thing we're not supposed to tell a young man when he grows up. It doesn't matter. You'll just have to forgive me for a while until I get used to you as a man of twenty, Lionel. My memory has a bad habit of getting lodged. I sometimes see things now the way they were before. For instance, I still can't believe you've already slept with a girl. When I try to think about it, all I can imagine is this little boy, wailing like the devil because he's wet his pants. You see, I can't get that picture of you out of my mind. But I suppose you are twenty and you have done it. That's why you're coming to Debrakot.

Before you get here, I should warn you. My wife takes all this very seriously, so you can expect her to be strict. She's not going to let you dash around with any of the girls up here. Probably she's told her friends about it, so I don't imagine they'll try to shove their daughters off on you. Women have an instinct for protecting their own kind. It's one of those things.

Your father said to put you to work. I will. We have an apple orchard which I started when we first moved here in 1946. Even though I've got two gardeners, it's too big a job for me. I'm getting old. Around town they call me 'bazurg sahib', which is like reminding a cocker spaniel that it has no tail. I'm all too well aware of it.

I'll explain the orchard to you when you get here. It's not a difficult job for a young man, even though there's a lot to be done.

Understand that I don't hold anything against you because of this mess you're into. It's natural. We all did it. Don't mind the women, they have to get upset over these things. When I was twenty, I did the same thing, only none of them that I know of got into trouble. For God's sake don't be embarrassed about it in front of me. I couldn't care less. Your father said it was a Hindu girl. I don't know which it's worse to get caught with, white, Muslim, or Hindu. For us, all three are a problem. Nobody wants his daughter in bed with someone until it's proper, and especially not with an Anglo-Indian. They think of us as illegitimate to begin with. The Indians will kill you if they get a chance. It's their country now. They can do as they please. I remember a friend of mine in the army by the name of Joey McChievers. He got a Muslim girl into trouble. Her family didn't dare touch Joey, because he was a British officer; they got his horse, though. When the syce was out exercising it in the maidan, four of the blighters attacked him. They made a mess of the poor animal. We had to shoot it. Now, I suppose they wouldn't hesitate to do the same to you.

I hope you like Debrakot. It might be too quiet for you after Lucknow, though that's why I think it's the nicest hill station. We don't have a motor road. All of the other places like Simla, Mussoorie, and Almora, they've got motor roads. The tourists pour in every summer and turn it into a bloody carnival. Nobody ever comes to Debrakot just to see it, even though it is pretty. We don't have a tourist season at all any more. It's too difficult to get here. In 'forty-six it was popular. It had a reputation for good air and a lot of people came up because of their health. At that time it was like any other hill station. Then, during partition, all of the Muslims moved out. Most of the shopkeepers used to be Muslim. When they left, a lot of Hindus took over, but by then it was already going downhill. They began to leave as soon as they got here. The other places had built their motor roads. Nobody came to Debrakot any more. It was too isolated. You'll see the bazaar. There are only a few shops left. Everything else is shut up tight. It's deserted. About ten years ago there was a rumour that they were finally going to build a road. A surveyor even came but we still can't drive a car up here and probably never will. I like it this way, even though all of the bungalows are falling apart and the chaukidars have taken over. They were hired to guard the houses and now they've brought in their cattle and turned the beautiful old homes into dirty cow sheds. The sahibs are gone for good. Who's going to complain?

With all best wishes. Sincerely yours,
Theodore Augden, Brig. Gen. (Rtd)

As my horse made its way up the narrow path, I tried to stop thinking about Lucknow and Sujeeta. I was tired of remembering but it was like trying to ignore her when she was in the same room. I couldn't forget her. It was like the time she woke before me and kissed me while I was sleeping. She tried not to disturb me but I woke anyway and in that brief moment when just your eyelids open, I saw her bent over me, with her lips on mine. She didn't realize I was awake. I closed my eyes quickly and pretended to still be asleep. Gently she kissed me. She played with my hair, murmuring so softly that I couldn't hear what she said. I lay there and tried to keep from moving. It was just like summer, when I take my bed outside and wake to the wind against my face. Finally I couldn't keep still any longer. I grabbed her. She squealed and then put a hand over her mouth. Nobody heard. We were in my room, which was on the roof. She hugged me and we laughed. I couldn't resist my memory of her.

'You looked like one of those old bulls that has gone to sleep in the shade,' she said.

'And you are the mynah that comes and pecks at my nose until I wake up.'

'I wanted to see whether it was time for me to go, but you were lying with your watch under you. I had to wake you up.'

'You can stay another hour. Look, it's only two o'clock. You've waked me for no reason,' I complained.

'Well, I didn't come here to sleep; I can do that in my own room,' she teased. 'You are such a huge bull and I am only a mynah. Why should you be so exhausted when I am wide awake?'

In college the word had it that Hindu girls were shy and scared. Everyone wanted an Anglo-Indian; they were supposed to be 'fast'. I've never known any girls other than Sujeeta.

At the sight of a new mountain peering over the shoulder of the one in front of it, I escaped out of my memory for a moment. It was as if everything was going to begin now, again, in a new place, removed from my past. I was ascending into a different world – the mountains, the forests. I had never been in thick forests before. The bridle path, after the first two miles, was submerged in the trees. I watched with amazement as the horse, the boy leading it, and I were suddenly dappled by the shadows and patches of light. The silence was that of a held breath. There was a damp, secretive atmosphere surrounding us; the oaks short, hunched beggars stretching out their branches like maimed arms. The ground was moss-covered and seemed alive. I suspected it would scuttle away if I touched it. The bird calls were different and I could never locate where they came from. Nothing was completely revealed – a moist secret – there was something concealed here – from out of the mouldering leaves and rotting wood sprang the new sprigs.

Father saw me off at the train station this morning. I said goodbye to Mother last night. She doesn't have her bed tea until ten and wouldn't get up before that if she had to. The train left at three. It's just as well, she would have become emotional and made a scene on the platform. I don't know whether she's more embarrassed or hurt by this whole affair. Maybe they're both the same thing to her. Anyway, she took it badly – a lot of crying – and telling my father to send me to England. She gets very melodramatic, as if she's a character in a Victorian play. She claimed that it wouldn't have happened if I'd gone to school 'back home'. I hate her saying that. I can't help it. I told her to stop calling England home. She's never been there. I told her it was crazy to dream that we'd ever been English. 'They've gone and left us, Mother,' I said.

At places the trees would fall away and the trail would climb across an open slope or along a cliff. Then I felt incredibly small, the hugeness of the mountains dwarfing me. Inside the forest I was big. I felt secure. Everything was smaller than me. But in the open, exposed to the mountains, I felt conspicuous, as if a great predatory bird was going to swoop down and pick me off the hillside like a flea.

I looked down at the boy walking beside me, holding the reins. He couldn't have been more than twelve but he walked with confidence and spoke like a man of twenty. He swaggered despite my attaché case, which he carried in his free hand. He wore a jaunty plastic hat, with a band of pink ribbon around it. Stuck in this was a marigold. It had wilted. The petals drooped, victims of the hot sun. The boy whistled a cinema tune as we went along. I had caught him staring at me a couple of times.

'What happened to you?' he finally asked. 'Were you in a fight?'

'Yes,' I said.

'The whole side of your face is purple. Does it hurt?'

He spoke in a dialect of the hills. I had trouble understanding.

'Not much now, but of course if I touch it . . .'

'What was it over?' he asked.

'Oh, nothing particular,' I lied. He did not ask me any more. I rode beside him, wrapped in my own silence.

Sujeeta and I met just about a year ago. It was my second term of college. I had passed the mid-year exams without any trouble. Classes had just begun again after the winter break. I was living at home, had only a few friends, and was cutting classes regularly. I would leave the house in the morning, expecting to go to the physics lecture or chemistry lab, but as soon as I was outside the day would seem too nice to waste in a stuffy room smelling of formaldehyde and pickled snakes. I would ride down to the river or over to the Residency and spend the day in the shade of a tree, reading novels or just loafing.

The Residency is a nice place, except for the memorials and plaques. During the mutiny it was where the British community in Lucknow holed up. All of the buildings are bombed out and ruined but there is still an atmosphere of grandeur about the place, if you're romantic enough to appreciate it. History had vacated the Residency, leaving it empty and silent. The gardens are beautiful. Everyone who's ever come and conquered India has built gardens. The Moguls brought trees from China and planted rose beds along their artificial streams and around their fountains. Out of the pale grey earth and saltpetre grew their secluded Edens – places to escape the dry heat and flat loneliness of the plains – where the caged finches sang their foreign songs and exiles dreamt of home. The English also built gardens, like those at the Residency, not as lavish.

Sujeeta was sitting on the lawn by one of the gardens. I rode past her three or four times before I finally stopped and wheeled my cycle over to where she was sitting. At first she was very rude to me, but after a while I got her talking. She even laughed at some of my jokes. I asked her to meet me again but she said it wouldn't be possible. She had failed the exams and had to study hard this term or else her father would take her out of college.

'You have been cutting too many classes,' I said.

'No, this is the first time.'

'Then maybe you haven't been cutting enough times. That can be just as bad, sometimes.'

Every day after that I went to the Residency hoping that she would be there. Finally on Sunday I found her inside one of the ruined rooms of the Resident's bungalow. She was dressed in a pastel-coloured sari and her thick hair was braided into a single strand. Her delicacy embarrassed me. I was wearing my old school blazer and tie. My hair was blown in every direction from the cycle ride; I was out of breath. My ears must have been red. I felt clumsy in front of her.

Sujeeta acted as if she hadn't expected me to come.

'Did you come here to see me?' I asked.

'No,' she answered, biting her lower lip and starting to leave.

'May I walk with you?'

'But if you leave your cycle here it will get stolen,' she said.

'I can lock it.'

She stepped past me and then turned.

'There is a banyan tree near the ruined Dance Hall. Do you know which one I mean? Come meet me there after ten minutes. No one will see us.'

I nodded.

'Do you want a Coca-Cola?' I yelled after her.

'Fanta, if they have it,' she cried back.

There was a small shop outside the gate. I had to pay the proprietor extra to let me take the bottles. I didn't argue. I felt like a boy who has just won a pocketful of marbles. Coming back, I rode without holding on to the handlebars. Leaning from side to side, I swerved through the clusters of tourists. A few of them shouted at me and called me reckless.

We sat with our backs against the tree and talked eagerly. Sujeeta discarded her shyness quickly. Her eyes never left my face, except when she would tell me something about herself. We did not talk seriously.

'You'll meet me here again, won't you?' I asked.

'Yes, Mr Lionel, sir!' she said, saluting.

'Why do you do that?' I asked. 'I'm not a military man.'

'But aren't you the British Resident here? I am just a poor native girl whom you found wandering around your garden. I amuse you. You will flirt and make passes at me and then go back inside to your white memsahib. She has blonde hair and such fair skin. Who am I, that you . . .'

I tried to laugh. I couldn't. I didn't want Sujeeta to see that I was hurt by her joke. She noticed, though, and stopped. I turned my head and looked away, angry at myself for being so sensitive.

'I'm sorry,' she said, touching my arm. 'I didn't think ... I shouldn't have said that. Don't be cross with me. Forgive me, Lionel.' She said my name slowly, trying to pronounce it correctly.

I turned around and glanced at her. She was biting her lip and looking as if she was going to cry.

'It's all right,' I said. 'Don't mind.' I put my hand against her cheek. My eyes wandered through the tendrils of the banyan tree. Sujeeta reached up and took my hand. She held it in both of hers. My skin was so white against hers, whiter than I had ever realized.

As we were sitting there, I remembered myself at ten asking, 'Mother, what am I, Indian or English?'

She said, 'You don't worry about that now, Lionel.'

Now, that barbed question tore at my mind again; it had always worried me, even before I was ten and had worked up the courage to ask her. She couldn't keep me from answering it this time. I had to.

I was confused and uncertain, like a child waking up in an unfamiliar room and finding itself alone. They've gone and left us. I'm scared. The room is dark. The window's in the wrong place. The sheets smell different. The door isn't where it should be.

Father ignores it. He's pretty dark anyway. But he married Mother. Why didn't he marry an Indian girl? He must have slept with dozens of them. I wonder how many brothers I really have besides Tony. My grandfather was pure English. He actually married a Bengali – my grandmother – in a cantonment church. It was a scandal but he didn't care; she was a Christian. Five years later he went to fight in France. He never came back. They couldn't stop him. Until she died, my grandmother believed he'd been killed in the war, though she was never notified. Finally Father wrote a letter to someone he knew, connected with the War Office, and found out that my grandfather had been honourably retired after the war and that his pension cheques were being cashed regularly. He told me this one night when he was drunk. That's when Father loosens up, 'and stops talking like an Indian', my mother says.

I asked Sujeeta many questions about her family. She never wanted to talk about them but I was curious and prodded her. She told me that her father had come to Lucknow after partition. He used to live in Rawalpindi. He lost everything in the looting. Some relatives in Lucknow helped him set up his business.

Soon we were meeting regularly. Sujeeta would sneak out at night and I would wait for her at the edge of the compound. We would rush to try and catch each other first and then stand by the gate a moment, trembling and excited in our danger, the hushed city intriguing to expose us, its whispers growing louder until we ran pursued through my mother's garden – its sweet familiar smell – then quietly up the stairs to my room, locking the screen behind us as we go in, shutting out the city and falling into the tiny universe of our embrace, squinting away everything around us, feeling nothing outside of ourselves, senseless and absorbed – each breath endless and important...

'Doesn't it ever bother you that you're refugees?' I asked.

'What does it matter?' she said. 'How can I remember something that happened before I was born? Would it make any difference to you if I was a Brahmin from Kerala or a Bengali? Would you prefer me if my grandfather had been English like yours?'

'No,' I said. 'But don't you ever wonder where you came from or who your family is?'

'Why? I'm here now, in a dark room with you. I don't even have my clothes on. It could be any time. It could be the Gupta age, or the Mauryan, or the Mughal Raj, or the British; it just happens that it is the Congress Raj. So what? You and I are outside of it. How do you know the Pandavas aren't fighting the Kuruvs right now on the other side of that door? The thing is that it doesn't matter. We're in our separate little room on the roof. The chaukidar is drunk. Your parents are asleep. Why should we let our grandfathers interrupt us with their history?' She buried her head in the pillow and began to laugh. 'I think I have been hearing too many lectures in college. Now I have begun lecturing myself,' she said.

Evening falls over Lucknow like a silk scarf. The fires are lit and phantoms of smoke circle above the flat roofs. Slowly they mingle, merging into one great haze, suspended ominously over the city. Kites begin to leave the air, pulled down by young boys, kings of their rooftop world. They have fought all day, cutting string after string, watching crippled opponents fall awkwardly out of the sky in the windborne war that goes on all spring. At dawn they rose like pennants and at dusk they descend, shivering in the gusty wind, torn at a corner perhaps, but nothing that can't be mended before bedtime.

Mother is in her garden, standing over the mali, telling him what to do. He is a new man and works nervously, keeping time with her words, his trowel stabbing into the ground as if he is killing someone. We never have the same mali for very long. They always quit. Mother yells at them too much and won't let anything be done when she's not there. During the day she will take a chair outside and watch the mali over her knitting. We have the best garden in Lucknow, people say. Mother is proud of it. It's more important to her than anything else. The house is always full of bouquets. When I was small she would take me through the garden and teach me all the names of flowers – nasturtiums, dahlias, cockscomb, baby's breath, sweetpeas. Those names are still there in my mind, like the names of my boyhood companions. But I have forgotten which is the hibiscus and whether dahlias are a monsoon flower or not, just as I have forgotten who was Dinesh and whether it was Neelu or Asha who wore ribbons in her hair.

I remember one year on Palm Sunday the compound children – my friends – raided Mother's flower beds. They tore the blossoms off their stalks and skewered them on the sharp points of their palm fronds. It was for the procession. There must have been at least two dozen of them, because the garden was completely trampled and many of the plants were torn up by their roots. The children came early, before we were up, and by the time someone heard them – the garden was ruined. I remember going out in my pyjamas, to have a look before breakfast. That was the only morning that Mother got up before eleven. She sat on the veranda overlooking the flower beds, drinking coffee and crying. The garden was what I imagined a battleground must look like, littered with the wounded and dying. Everyone in the compound came to see what had happened. It was very solemn. Their eyes would first scan the scattered petals, the bent and broken stalks, and then glance over to the veranda, where Mother sat mourning like the great widow. All of my friends got a beating that night and didn't dare come near the house for another week. Mother screamed at the mali more than ever as they worked frantically, trying to rescue as much as they could by Easter. She nursed it back to its usual opulence and the mali had to quit afterwards, because of an ulcer.

The gate swings slowly open towards me with a rasping moan. I step outside and into the wide shadow of the wall where I always wait for Sujeeta, sitting on the stack of extra bricks left over and never removed after the wall was built. The darkness is complete, except for the moon, which is no more than a pale slit in the sky. There is too much dust haze to see the stars.

Sujeeta is late. I sit staring into the darkness, hoping to catch the glint off her bangles. She never uses a torch and comes by a dark route, through the unlit streets and across the open lot behind the compound. Sometimes a pariah dog will bark at the edge of the field but usually she arrives without warning.

That night Sujeeta brought something with her. It was a small cage. She put it on top of my dresser and removed the covering. Inside was a parakeet, its rose-coloured head cocked to one side.

'Is it yours?' I asked.

'My sister's,' she said, opening the wire door and putting her hand inside. The bird hopped onto it eagerly and ducked as she brought it out.

I reached over to pet it. The parakeet snapped its head around and in a phlegmy voice cried, 'Bloody fool!'

I know that I jumped and my face must have showed my astonishment, because Sujeeta began to laugh hysterically. The parakeet left her hand and flew over to the window sill.

'He talks,' I said, bewildered.

'Of course, we taught him to.'

'Does he say anything else?'

'A few things,' Sujeeta said, turning and calling, 'Come here, Mitthu, recite something for Lionel.' The bird strutted along the sill like a little general, his long tail dragging behind him. Sujeeta put her hand out and he jumped onto it.

'Now, tell Lionel your name,' she commanded.

'Bloody fool!' screeched the parakeet.

'What does your mother do when she hears him swear?' I asked.

'She doesn't know what it means. Besides, my brother taught him that, not us.'

'Come, Mitthu,' I said, 'give us a lecture.'

'He looks like a professor, doesn't he, a real snob,' said Sujeeta. 'Lionel, do you have a mirror?'

'There's a big one on the dresser.'

'No, a small hand mirror.'

'I think so,' I said. It was in the first drawer I looked in. Sujeeta took Mitthu and set him down on the bedstead. Slowly she brought the glass up in front of him. He twisted his head around and looked at his reflection for a moment, clicking his fat tongue like a disapproving auntie.

'Recite your poem,' said Sujeeta.

'Bloody fool!' cried the parakeet.

I began to laugh again. Sujeeta tapped him angrily on the beak with her finger and scolded him. He answered back with a long string of abusive squawks and screeches. After their argument was over, she tried again. But Mitthu refused to say anything other than 'Bloody fool'.

Sujeeta finally gave up and put him back in his cage.

'It's because he's in a new place. Otherwise, he loves to recite his poem. I wish my brother hadn't taught him to swear. He likes it more than anything else. It's because he's a male,' she said with a smirk.

'How did you teach him?'

'With a mirror. You hold it up in front of him and he's such a snob that it absorbs his attention. When you say something he thinks it's his reflection talking and tries to repeat it. If we left the mirror in his cage he'd admire himself all day.'

'Maybe he thinks it's his sweetheart.'

'That could be. His poem is very romantic.'

'You recite it,' I said.

'No, I've got a better idea,' Sujeeta said, taking me by the shoulders and turning me around. 'I'll teach it to you.'

She brought the mirror up in front of me and held it there. All I could see was my face leering back at me. I was embarrassed and averted my eyes. When I looked up again I noticed that my hair needed combing. Instinctively I ran my hand through it. Sujeeta began to laugh.

'See, you're just as much of a snob as Mitthu. I didn't put this mirror up in front of you so that you could primp. Just look at yourself, you're not all that beautiful.'

I stared back at the mirror self-consciously, trying to look past the reflection. It was impossible. My own eyes followed me. I was forced to look at myself. After a while I got used to it and actually began to study my own face. Before that I had never seen myself for more than an instant, averting my eyes from the glass except when it was necessary. It's the same when I meet a person. I can never look at them. Sujeeta always complained that I didn't look at her.

Sheeshee bharee gulab se, toree nahin jatee,
Dill mayree, bharee pyar se, Khalee nahin hotee.

'Repeat that,' Sujeeta said. 'The bottle of rose water is never broken. My heart, filled with love, is never emptied.'

'Bloody fool!' I said, trying to imitate Mitthu.

'*Areh*, tonight I am stuck with two idiots. I should have known this would happen. Two parakeets in the same cage always copy each other.'

'Bloody fool!' I squawked again, grabbing Sujeeta around the waist. She brought the mirror up between us and my reflection confronted me again.

Taking the mirror, I moved it a little so that it caught Sujeeta's reflection off the large mirror on top of the bureau. She had her arms around me and her chin resting on my shoulder. We made a face at each other and smiled. I didn't avert my eyes this time or look at her hands or lean over to kiss her. We just returned each other's reflection. Her eyes followed mine exactly, as if I was looking at myself in the mirror. We tried to imitate each other. She wrinkled up her nose and so did I. I stuck out my tongue and she stuck out hers. I puffed my cheeks and she mimicked me. Sujeeta hugged me tightly, pulling me as close to her as she could. I tossed the mirror onto the bed and kissed her. We stood still for a moment, as if there was only one of us. I raised my hands to her face and pulled it away from mine. It seemed as if I had the mirror in my hands again. We looked at each other like reflections.

My eyes climb to the mountains again, searching for familiarity, something to recognize. There is no fear in me; there is no place for it. I am crammed full of other thoughts and worries, each one crying out for my attention. And yet, though there is no room, there is a huge vacancy.

The last time I saw her, it was no different from any of those other times. I expected to see her the next week. When she didn't come, I wandered through the city, searching for her. Perhaps she saw me from her window but didn't dare call out, for fear that they would catch me. I didn't know where she was. If I'd known, I would have found her. At least I could have heard the truth from her. But she was swallowed up by the city. She became a part of its mystery. They have their medicines for these things. I hope it doesn't kill her. She will be kept locked up from now on. Her father will keep her out of college. They will marry her off quickly before the rumours spread, and if her husband is simple enough to believe that she is a virgin, it will be all right. This is the end she had expected and she would have wanted us to separate as we did that last night, unaware of it ending.

From each part of the city the Mullas begin to wail through crackling amplifiers, calling the faithful to the fifth prayer of the day. Soon it will be Moharram. The Sunnis and Shias will grow angry, the city will be tense, and we will see police everywhere. Tonight, though, it is quiet, muted by the smoke, dulled by the lethargy of evening. The streets mutter contentedly with the sounds of traffic.

I lean on the parapet outside my room listening to mynahs in the neem tree, my younger brother shouting at his companions, the servant's boys. One of his old kites – a bamboo skeleton and torn tissue paper, lying at my feet, too damaged to repair. I hear the soft rustle of pigeons nesting in the chinks, finally safe from my brother's catapult, which Father confiscated because Tony broke the bulb outside old Mrs Kennedy's house. Now he is making a new one, which he says will be even better. Evenings are always lonely except when there are games to finish.

'We should leave Lucknow,' I said. 'Go some place where we don't have to be secretive.'

'Where?' asked Sujeeta.

'To Calcutta maybe. I know people there.'

'And what are they going to do when you show up with a Hindu girl? They'll call me your pigeon and laugh behind our backs. You don't even have your degree. What will you do? It's like wanting to marry me. Why do you fool yourself, thinking about these things?'

'But, Sujeeta, how can you come here every week without

looking forward to a time when we won't have to hide? Don't you ever look ahead?'

'No, I try not to. If I did, all I'd see would be a time when we are separated. It's better to be happy that I am with you now, than sad because a year or two years from now you'll be taken away.'

'What do you mean, I'll be taken away?'

'Lionel, it's impossible. I am the daughter of a Baniya and I will marry a Baniya. How can we run away from it? You have to marry among your own people too. But let's not worry about it. Unless you would rather I went away now, having told you this.'

'Of course not. It's just that I look forward to things. I dream about what I'm going to do, but because I'm dreaming about it now, you are a part of my dreams. I imagine that you'll be with me forever because right now the future is only in my mind. It hasn't come yet and when it does maybe it will be different but until then you have to be in it with me. My mind can't escape the present. Do you understand what I mean?'

'No,' said Sujeeta, with a smile. 'Forget about it, though.'

The city is a labyrinth of gullies and twisted streets. From the roof I can see it spread out, fading into the smoke. The electricity blinks on and everything goes crazy for a moment like one of those machines that tell your weight and fortune, it is blinding and dizzy. But these are the bazaars, like Garbarjhala, where Sujeeta's father has his shop. There are other sections of the city where it is still dark except for an occasional yellow bulb – the residential areas, separated from the rest of the city, where the electricity isn't turned on until the men come home, places of silence and mystery within the chaos – the eye of the storm. Only those who live there can find their way through the gullies they grew up in. If a stranger wanders in by mistake, he will feel eyes upon him from behind the barred windows. Children will surround him with shouts. There will be the smell of mustard oil and frying spices. The dogs will run at him, teeth bared.

From her window, Sujeeta could climb onto the wall of the courtyard and then lower herself into the street. I never saw her house but she described it to me. She and her two sisters shared a room. They were both younger than Sujeeta and did not say anything when she went out at night. One time her mother came into their room while Sujeeta was with me. They had fixed the bed so that it looked as if she was in it. The youngest sister acted sick and asked if she could sleep with her mother for the rest of the night. That saved us.

Her fragrance each time was different. I would try to guess what it was. Roses, jasmine, champak, sandalwood, or rat-kirani? Usually it was a flower I had never heard of. She would tell me where there was a bush of it and promise to take me there some day. Before meeting her I had never appreciated odours. Our house had always smelled of boot polish and mothballs in the closets and Mother's lavender perfume. I was so used to the familiar scents that I had forgotten them. I used to like the smell of Mother's garden. It was a hot sweet smell, a mixture of all the flowers. But I had never realized their variety before, that each one had its separate fragrance.

The first night we met at the gate, I didn't mention to Sujeeta that I liked her perfume. I didn't want to offend her. Smell, Mother taught me, was an embarrassing sense. You could look at a person, even touch them, but never admit that you smelled them. There's something animal about it and people don't like to be doggy with each other. It disgusts them. That first night, though, I was fascinated. I wanted to know which flower it was, and finally, after three or four weeks, I felt confident enough to ask her.

'Magnolia,' she said.

'And last week?'

'Lotus, I think.'

'What perfume is it?' I asked.

'They call it *ittar*. Here in Lucknow, there is a group of people that produce it. They can make any perfume you want, even onion and cucumber. They make one that smells like the earth just after it has rained. Tell me what flower is your favourite and I will wear it for you. They make anything. Now, because it is spring, most of the perfume is rose-scented. They go from place to place; wherever there is a garden with the flower they want, these people set up their factory and make it. Do you like roses?'

I nodded.

She was the flower, opening her delicate petals slowly as I watched, unfolding herself and revealing her mysterious intricacies before me – a strange flower, emitting an odour of fascination such as a perfumer dreams of in his idleness, the ambition of bringing lovers together by discovering the scent of seduction – but he is a pedlar of fragrances and must reproduce the smell of corn for the farmer, he must duplicate the sour odour of silver, gold, and paper to set the nose of usury quivering; he would steal like a thief into the lovers' bedroom, just as he hunts out each flower in its season, and set up his factory there, hoping to capture a perfume which suggests their passion – I escaped myself like a bee leaving its hive, to search for new blossoms.

I had always said that I was Indian. I could talk Hindi better than even Tony. I thought I understood things I saw in town and was happy when someone would ask if I came from Kashmir, because of my fair skin. But knowing Sujeeta made me realize how different I was. Things like her perfume proved how little I knew outside of myself and my family. It was frustrating. I was really no different from my mother with her lavender scent, her talcum powder complexion, and her gin and lime before dinner. I was an Anglo-Indian and nothing would erase it. Even in my room at night, with the curtains drawn and the lights out, my body was pale. Sujeeta liked the colour of my skin and often she would get up and run into a dark corner. She would say, 'See how I disappear, and you can't. I'll never lose you.'

It was completely dark now. Tony and his friends had brought their game of marbles into the apron of yellow light cast by the veranda bulb. It was an eerie brightness, which projected dark shadows and extended in a half-circle around their hunkered shapes. It had a definite perimeter beyond which there was darkness. The bulb had been there as long as I could remember. Somehow it had escaped Tony's catty and never seemed to burn out. I stood immediately above it, in shadow. Tony and his friends shifted about like sand crabs, absorbed in their game.

I heard voices at the compound gate, arguing with the watchman. After a few minutes there was the sound of footsteps coming along the drive. Three men strode into the illuminated area below me, followed by the chaukidar, carrying his night stick helplessly. He was pleading with them. They wore plaid lungis and loose shirts with the sleeves rolled up. Tony and his friends stopped their game and moved aside. The three men walked up to the veranda door and knocked. Without waiting, they went in. The watchman followed. I heard the front door open and my mother say something.

There was a gruff reply. Her voice became shrill. She was using all of the Hindi she knew, a string of abusive half-phrases. Her voice was like a high pathetic bark. Occasionally the men's voices broke in, husky and impatient. Without seeing it, I could picture the scene perfectly. The watchman's voice rose above the others'. He was an old man, gaunt and tubercular. He told them to leave or else he would go for help. A minute later one of the three appeared, dragging him out of the house like a dead cat. He took him outside the circle of light and left him there. The old man groaned and rolled over onto his face. Tony and his friends retreated into the shadow of a jasmine bush. The watchman's foot protruded awkwardly into the hemisphere of light. It looked like a stage below me. I had the feeling of being in a theatre, watching a macabre drama. On the left lay the watchman, practically obscured in darkness. Across from him, and also in the shadows, crouched my brother and his friends. The voices continued inside, my mother's brittle and sharp like broken glass. It wasn't fear that kept me from going downstairs to help her; it was an awful hypnosis. I felt like an actor, placed on a stage and immobile until a cue sets him into motion. I could picture it so vividly: Mother sitting in her favourite stuffed chair, waiting for my father, a little drunk – three gin and tonics in her by now, almost dinner time. Her first reaction to the men would be haughty, disguising her fear. When finally her composure broke, the lines of her face snarled into a frightened grin, revealing her yellow teeth. It was the grin of an animal facing its predator. That was when she started to scream, swearing at them in Hindi, her own peculiar Hindi, screaming at them to get out of her house. The three men just stood there scowling and repeating something to her which she was too excited to try to understand. I heard the kitchen door slam and the sound of someone running. The cook had gone out, either to save himself or to bring help. I still couldn't move; it was so clear in my mind. The sight of it held me there. Mother was facing the three men with all of the hatred and bitterness she had pent up. It must have frustrated her, their three dark faces staring back disdainfully. She hated the sight of their bare brown arms and shirts open over their black chests. She hated their swarthy faces and oily hair, their black eyes looking right into her. She stood there grinning, her blouse buttoned right down to the wrists of her trembling hands and all the way up her throat. My fingers clutched the parapet. I stood perfectly still in the warm shadows of the roof, like a fly on the rim of a glass, listening to her screams and watching my brother whispering to his friends. One of them broke away from the bush and took off running down the drive. He disappeared out the gate. Suddenly the voices grew louder; beneath me the door swung open. The three men stepped out into the light. One of them held my mother by the arm. They walked to the centre of the stage and stopped. One of them, a man with twirled moustaches, stepped ahead of the others; like a ringmaster facing an audience, he shouted, 'Come here, bhanchut! I'll teach you who to fornicate with!' Over his voice, I heard my mother's scream. 'Lionel!' The man who held her laughed and grabbed her by the hair, pulling her head back until she was looking up into his squinting eyes. Suddenly I heard myself answering her. 'Here I am, Mother. I'm the one they want.' The three men turned and looked up at the roof. The bulb blinded them. They shielded their eyes and tried to find me behind the glare. I came down by the steps. Tony was watching me. I could see his eyes and his pale legs beneath his khaki half-pants. The men stood where they were as I came into the yellow skirt of light. I felt like a night moth attracted by the bulb, unwillingly flying into it. Stepping from the shadows into its brightness, I felt suddenly exposed. There was no sound except for the distant murmur of the city. I walked slowly to the centre, stopping a few feet away from Sujeeta's brother. I could smell alcohol on his breath. Mother was shaking her head and looking at me in horror. Her eyes were dark and sunken, as if they'd been burned into her powdered face. Her makeup was streaked into two black lines down her cheeks. It was as if the crying had washed off her white complexion and revealed something beneath it, the darkness of her skin. After a second of hesitation, Sujeeta's brother lunged at me. I tried to duck, covering myself with an arm, but he caught me awkwardly on the side of the head with his right hand open. There was a sharp explosion. Mother screamed again; I felt his body landing on top of me. I could smell him. He was a dark tangle of arms. I didn't fight back. His fist hit my cheek and glanced off. When it came back again it slammed into my mouth. I could feel the teeth break. I turned my head and tried to spit. This time his fist dug into my ear. My face was pushed into the gravel.

My tongue was numb and swollen. I tried to swallow. There was a lot of dirt in my mouth, and blood. I could see it on the ground, spattered like rose petals under a bush. In the yellow light it was a different colour – a sickly orange. Grabbing my hair and twisting my head towards him, he hit me two or three more times. When he pulled me around I caught a glimpse of Tony's scared eyes watching me. He was helpless. I tried to look at him and tell him that it was all right, that I knew he couldn't do anything. I was hit above the eye, so that the blood came down and collected in the corner and streaked down my cheek like tears. I tried to say something, but all that came out was a rasping gurgle. Then he was off me. I could hear his voice and tried to look up at him. The light was glaring in my eyes. I felt a wad of spittle land on my neck. I raised a hand in front of me. It was like looking at the sun during an eclipse. My hand hung there above my head as if it wasn't mine, a jaundiced hand with long fingers, the veins and tendons standing out. It was separate from me, someone else's, it seemed. I felt no particular pain, except a dull agony flowing to every part of my body, like a poison. It was as if his hatred had been transfused into me. I could taste it in my mouth. Mother was watching me now with an almost benign look on her face. For a moment I thought she had fainted but then I saw her blink. Her lips were moving gently, she was muttering something. All of the emotion had left her face. His foot dug into my stomach. I tried to turn away but he kicked me in the groin. I stared out into the darkness, beyond the yellow circle, beyond the apparitions surrounding me. There was the chaukidar's leg a few feet away and his crooked form stretched into the shadows. There was nothing to reach for, no place to crawl into. When I was small and Mother would beat me, I'd climb into the closet and sit among the shoes, surrounded by coats and the familiar smell of boot polish and mothballs. Now there was nowhere I could escape to. There was only the gravel of the drive, yellow and empty. Beyond that there was only the darkness.

I don't know how I got there. I remember hearing shouts and seeing torch beams waving in the darkness. I must have crawled over the chaukidar and dragged myself into the garden, though I remember none of it. I got as far as the sweet peas, my head pressed against the chicken wire and my shoulders hunched around my neck. Tony was pulling me out of the flower bed when I came to my senses. He kept saying that it was all right, that they'd caught the men. I lay there, my head in the soft earth, Tony wiping off my face and saying things. I could smell the flowers, all of their fragrances mixed together. Mother came and knelt down beside me. 'It's all right now, Lionel. You're safe now. It's all right.' She stroked my hair frantically. The scent of lavender perfume and the strong odour of the garden overwhelmed me. Though I tried, I could no longer remember what a lotus smelled like or what was different about the odour of champak.

'On which of these hills is Debrakot?' I asked.

'Can't you see it there?' said the boy, pointing his finger. 'Just behind that hill with the two lone pine trees.'

Two ridges, like a pair of great thighs, curved gradually down into the narrow valley. Debrakot appeared to huddle between them, scattered and lonely. At the first sight of it I felt instinctively that I was returning home – nostalgia, after an absence earlier than my recollection. I was born here and had lived here for a year as a baby. Nothing specific was familiar, yet all together, the red tin roofs, the whitewashed walls, and crooked paths, the smell of pines, the cow bells ringing on the slopes below me, all these things were distantly familiar. I couldn't distinguish the feeling any more than to say it was the atmosphere. Perhaps it was because Mother had told me about Debrakot. She had always liked the hills and hated Lucknow because of the heat, she said, though I have never seen her affected by summer, even the worst summer. She tries very hard to suffer and won't accept invitations between the first of May and the beginning of the rains. It is all a façade, though, like the talcum powder and the lavender perfume.

I turned to the boy again. 'Where is the havagarh?' I asked.

'Just up ahead from here, half a mile. Do you see where the road seems to climb? It is around that corner, in the gap.'

The havagarh was a round, cement pavilion, open on all sides. It had been painted red at one time. As we came in sight of it, I saw a figure stand up. It could only have been the Brigadier. He stood erectly, despite his age and enormous weight. You could tell immediately that he was military, perhaps because of the way his head was cocked back a little on his neck like the hammer of a revolver, or perhaps because of the way his legs were spread.

'Hello, Lionel. How are you? Good to see you.'

We shook hands. I paid the boy off and walked over to the pavilion. Brigadier Augden was pouring out a cup of coffee for me from a thermos. Behind the havagarh stood two ponies and their syce, a short stout man with a greying beard. He was perfectly matched to the ponies. His head was on a level with theirs and when they moved he would whisper something and stroke their necks with his sturdy hands.

'My God,' said the Brigadier, 'did one of them do that to your face?'

'Yes, the girl's brother.'

'Well, I suppose you're lucky. He could have done worse.'

I nodded.

We drank our coffee and then rode the mile and a half on to Debrakot.

TWO . *Palm and Pine*

1 . Cairo

Except for an occasional rooftop or the exposed corner of a veranda, the old bungalows are buried in the forest. The oaks, the deodars, the pines enclose Debrakot and shelter it. It is a lost town, removed from the government survey maps ten years ago. We have taken refuge here, hiding from the rest of the towns and cities which remain spots of ink on the map. The forest and the mountains absorb us and keep our secrets.

I have always hated India, not because I loved England. No, the English love this country and hated to let go of it. But I am not English. Nor am I an Indian. I am not definitely one or the other – and not a third either. The history books make sweeping statements: 'The English took women from among the natives and there was much interbreeding.' It makes you think of flies on a pond, laying their eggs and spawning generations in unison. No, I am the product of a solitary copulation performed not for my sake but to slake my father's desire. Each of us is nothing more than that.

From when I was a boy I wanted a uniform – a British uniform. I became an officer by working up from the bottom. It's not an easy way to do it but I have always had an eye for the difficult. All along the way I kept expecting someone to stop me and say, 'You're a half-caste. It stops here for you. Get off the train.' But then suddenly I was a subaltern for something I did in the NWFP.

From there it was a hop, skip, and a jump to becoming a Captain. I went on up from there but I still wanted to leave India.

The few of us who were called Eurasians first and officers afterwards were looked on by the Brits as upstarts. The Indians called us snobs. We didn't know our ass from our tits what was going on. We drank our b. and s. at the club and tried to flirt with Englishwomen. But in the end it was a couple of glasses of desi sharab and a Hindu pross that kept us grinning. Though I thought for a while that my uniform made me an Englishman at last.

But it was hardly that easy. There was always fights and hard words between us and the rest. I thought it was the country. The Brits were jealous of India and they must have thought we were taking it away from them. They could keep it as far as we were concerned. I dreamed of leaving the place, of going abroad to China and Greece, where nobody knew who I was and I could be English. Not that I really cared what I was, so long as I was something.

I was attached to an armoured div. which went to Egypt during the first year of the war. It was what I had wanted for years – a chance to escape the country which had borne me. Finally I was going to leave behind the bitterness and jealousy of India. My transfer left me completely anonymous and when I arrived in Egypt it seemed as if no one knew me or who I was.

Our ship crossed from Bombay to Aden. I promised myself as we steamed out of the harbour that I would never come back. The Gateway to India receded into the horizon. The huge arch and massive shape stood as a reminder that England was jealous of this country, and those who entered it entered through her monument. For me it was a gateway too. It opened onto a new world. I was issuing out of India, hoping never to come back again. I stood on deck until dinner was served, watching the coastline grow faint and disappear.

At Port Said there was nothing but confusion, a hot sweaty confusion of stevedores, shipping agents, Egyptians, Copts, Arabs, French, English, cab drivers, and all varieties of urchins, pickpockets, and loafers. I was swept off the ship. 'Effendi, Effendi . . . luggage, I will carry.' – 'No, Effendi, I will carry, only one pound.' – 'Hotel? Effendi?' There was the smell of the canal, a bitter smell which comes from the mixture of oil and water. There was the smell of the desert, which I would soon recognize. Even the sun had a smell, hot and oily. It was all foreign and though I was pestered by porters I was happy and enjoyed being part of the confusion. Broken English, French, Arabic, and dialects all garbled together so that it sounded as though the crowd was speaking gibberish.

'Major Augden?'

I stopped and turned around to see who had spoken. A stout English sergeant with sandy hair and squinted eyes saluted me. I saluted back.

'Just arrived from Bombay, sir?'

'That's right.'

'I'm to take you to Cairo, sir.'

I nodded as he lifted my suitcase and ordered a boy to carry my trunk. We walked for a few minutes and finally escaped the crowd. The sergeant helped the boy stow the trunk in the back of a jeep. We rode out of the city with the boy squatting silently on the trunk and the jeep jumping along the rough road.

'Bloody hot, sir.'

'Yes, it is.'

'Do they have deserts in India, sir?'

'In some places,' I said. The boy sat looking backwards and saying nothing.

'All this bloody, bloody sand,' said the sergeant. 'You know, sir, I was thinking; I have a plan. If we could rig up enough wind machines, like fans with rotors and screws, so that they'd produce a regular hurricane what would blow all this bloody sand into the air, we could blow it right across the Mediterranean and cover Italy, Germany, and France just so as to be safe. Why, that would end the war. Move the Sahara, sir. They could call the Rhine the Nile, sir. All this bloody sand.'

I laughed to be polite.

Two hours later: 'That's the citadel over Cairo, sir. The mosque of Muhammad Ali. Impressive, isn't it, sir?'

'Yes, it is. Have you ever been to India, Sergeant?'

'No, sir, and I don't think I'd like to go.'

'Why not?'

'It'd be bloody awful, all those wogs and babus.'

*

Even with the war going on, Cairo had a festive atmosphere. I took a room at the Hotel Cleopatra until there was a place for me in the cantonment.

The first night I had dinner brought to my room and watched the sun setting over the Pyramids. Their sharp geometric shapes rising out of the desert had an eerie effect on the landscape, as if the jungle of crowded houses which stretched below me was a regression into a bestial civilization and the Pyramids with their straight uncorrupted lines stood for a lost dignity. The war, too, seemed harsh and barbarous, hovering on the horizon. I imagined the tanks and armoured cars churning through endless sand dunes, and felt a brutal loneliness. But somehow I enjoyed the feeling. India seemed so far away and safe on its peninsula. I was eager for the fighting and the excitement of the strange city. Sitting in front of the low table spooning soup into my mouth, I felt a surge of independence. It was what a lion must feel when it escapes from a circus.

That night I wandered down to the river where the casinos are arranged in the open air, cafés where the soldiers and other men of the city mingle, talking softly about the war and their fortunes over thimble-sized cups of coffee. I took a table by myself as close to the water as I could get. It flowed like black oil, reflecting the light from the casinos as it swept past. I ordered tea. The waiter looked at me curiously. I changed my order to coffee. He realized I was new to Cairo but did not know where from.

I had my head turned, watching the river, when the chair across from me was pulled back with a screech and a tall man in a bulging suit lowered himself into it.

'My name's Charley Carter, mind if I join you?'

I guessed he was American.

'Major Augden,' I said, offering my hand.

'Where do you come from?'

I fumbled a little but then said, 'India.'

'Is that so?'

A feeling of exposure ran through me. Suddenly I felt he knew who I was. But then I realized he couldn't have guessed.

'When are you English going to get out of that country?' He didn't know. It reassured me.

'Oh, we'll be there for a long time yet.'

'I'm interested in India, as a journalist.'

'For no other reason?'

'It sounds like a place I'd enjoy,' he said. 'Hey, is it true what I hear about this pig-sticking?'

'What about it?'

'I mean, do you really chase around on horses and spear boars?'

'Oh, yes,' I said. The waiter brought my coffee. I took a sip and made a face.

'You don't like the coffee?'

'No,' I said.

'Order something else,' said Carter, reaching over and picking up my coffee. He drank it in a swallow and grinned.

'You must have quite a stomach.'

'Genuine cast-iron Chicago pot-belly,' he said, slapping his sides. 'I can eat ten franks and mustard, sauerkraut, fries and ketchup, three cups of coffee, and an apple without a belch.'

'I beg your pardon?'

'It's our version of pig-sticking, forget it. When did you get to Cairo?'

'This morning.'

'Where are you staying?'

'The Cleopatra.'

'I know where that is.'

Carter and I became friends. He was covering the desert war for 'a rinky-dink midwestern newspaper'. Carter was different from anyone I'd met before. He was rude and noisy but a good fellow. When I talked about scotch, he talked about bourbon. He thought I was English and I didn't say anything about it. It wouldn't have mattered if he'd known that I was of mixed blood. I felt suddenly released from India and unselfconscious. We met again two nights later at the same casino. He took me to another place up the river, through some of the older streets, into a sinister café where a dark-eyed girl was dancing on a naked stage. She was black-haired and her eyes were rimmed with kajal. Her lips were full and pouted as she danced. She had a high skirt on and a tiny glittering brassière. We nudged our way through a crowd of Egyptians and took a table right in front of her. An old man was playing an oud and a younger man slapped a tambourine against his leg in time to her dance.

There was an English officer in the café. He stared at me. It wasn't a face I recognized but it seemed to recognize me. We didn't say anything to each other, though we sat only a couple of tables apart. Our eyes shifted back and forth. The girl was writhing her pelvis around like a snake that had broken its back. Carter was enjoying himself, whistling at her and shouting out for her to take her brassière off. The English officer was sipping coffee. As he watched me a sneer broke on his lips and then vanished. I felt uncomfortable. He seemed to be judging me. In the yellow glare of the café his face was broken into light and shadow, with stark outlines. There was something evil about him and I tried to ignore the man but when I looked away his eyes burned through me. Memories of India poured into me. The dancing girl seemed distant and unreal as I remembered the fights I'd had with Englishmen over train compartments, bar stools, horses, and women. They fought with a hatred which I could not understand. My instincts and my stubbornness lashed out at them, protecting myself and my pride. It was my pride against their hatred.

The Englishman got up and came towards me but then went past and out the door. As he went by me he gave me a push with the palm of his hand and I could feel the hatred in his touch. I did not fight with him or even say anything. He was outside before I realized what he had done. The girl danced on but I could not concentrate on her overripe body, quivering with the dance. My thoughts glassed me in and she was like a moth battering against a window pane. Carter watched and was oblivious of the Englishman.

Did he know me? Had we met in India once? I could not recall his face.

I got quarters in Ma'adi, the cantonment, and settled in. Our division was kept ready but we did not go into the war for a long time. It continued deep in the desert and even the sound of the guns did not reach us. We waited impatiently for our chance to fight. Until then Cairo entertained us like kings. We roamed the casinos and cafés, rode camels and bought horses. Every day I was mistaken for an Englishman and that pleased me. The bartenders, orderlies, and peons all treated me like a Brit. It flattered me and I worked hard at erasing all of my Anglo-Indian phrases and accent.

But all the time the face of the officer haunted me and I was afraid to meet him. I was not scared of fighting him but I was afraid that it would expose me and show everyone who I was.

Carter and I spent most of our free time together. One day we rode out to the Pyramids on our horses. I had bought a lovely Arab, the colour of the desert with a blonde mane and nostrils which flared open in excitement. It walked through the sand with haughty steps, lifting its hooves high as it shook its head. There was defiance in its eye and it took me three weeks to get it used to me.

'That's a thoroughbred all right,' said Carter. 'Cross-breeding kills a horse's spirit.'

'Yes, this horse has an arrogance,' I said.

As we were circling one of the Pyramids, I noticed another rider cantering towards us. He was coming out of the sun and I didn't recognize him until he was a short distance away. Carter waved. The man sat erect in his saddle and made no reply. It was the same Englishman. He stopped a few yards away, his horse snorting and stamping its hooves.

'I said hello,' Carter shouted.

The Englishman didn't even look at him.

'Chee-chee,' he said, and tossed his head. I pulled my horse around.

'What did you say?' I asked.

'Chee-chee,' he said again.

My Arab was on edge, and when he felt my heels clutch his ribs, he leapt forward. The Englishman's horse was startled and shied violently. Its rider tried to hold on but lost his grip and fell off into the sand. He shouted after us but we walked our horses around the Pyramid slowly and left him there.

'Strange bastard,' said Carter.

'Cheeky blighter.'

'What did he call you?'

'I'm not sure. I didn't catch it.' Carter was confused but still didn't seem to have guessed. I hoped he wouldn't ask any more questions.

Three nights later we were sitting at a casino playing cards with two other friends. It was a quiet night and not many of the tables were filled. I noticed the Englishman before he saw us. He glanced around almost as if he were looking for me. Our eyes met and we stared at each other for a few minutes.

I laid my cards down on the table and excused myself. Walking up to the man, I looked him over.

'May I know your name?'

'Why do you want to know that, you bloody half-and-half?'

'So as to know who it was I knocked off his horse.'

He threatened to hit me. He had been drinking but not enough to make him clumsy.

'Shall we settle this outside?' I said.

He turned and went out the door. I followed him. As soon as we were in the shadows of the street, he spun around and hit me hard on the jaw. I went down. As I lay in the dust of the street and let my eyes clear, I heard him running away like a scared rabbit.

A month later we were all in the war for real. Carter followed a story into the Sahara and was killed. I suppose the English officer was also called into the fighting. Perhaps he was killed, for that was the last I heard of him.

I knew after he hit me that I really was what he had called me, that I would never escape India, that no place would hide me. After the war a ship took me back down the canal, now a Lieutenant Colonel. The Gateway to India stood as firmly as it had before and I returned to the country I hated.

Over the years Debrakot has become more and more secluded. It has hidden me so that I can almost forget who I am. Certainly others have forgotten me. It is quiet but, more than that, Debrakot protects us.

2 . *Latif*

Latif shaves me every morning. He wakes me and then washes my face. He lathers my jowls until they are white with soap. I lie motionless under the covers as he whets the flat, white blade on a strap and then passes it over my cheeks neatly, scraping away soap and beard, leaving only the smooth, pitted skin beneath. His fingers move precisely, making my face taut at places, loosening it at others. All the time I lie there like an imbecile child. Every morning I take the mirror in both my hands and inspect his work. Latif knows me well. His fingers contain a knowledge of my face, my moods, my thoughts. He has seen me look at myself in a mirror. A man reveals himself to his own reflection.

He is my servant, not my wife's. Hers are different. Latif does only two things. He shaves me and grooms my horses, in that order. If he rubbed down the horses first, his hands would smell.

While I dress, he goes out to the stables and rubs down Elphinstone. He saddles the horse and leads him out to the road, where they wait for me. Elphinstone is always nervous, biting the air and kicking the ground. When I appear Elphinstone grins and tries to run towards me. We ride for two hours every day.

My wife's servants are all Hindus. They do not like Latif and are jealous of him. He is a Muslim from Hyderabad. I hired him in 'forty-five, just before I was married. He was twenty-seven then, bright and arrogant with a fringe of beard along his jaw.

A year later I bought the orchard and bungalow in Debrakot and moved my wife up there. In those days the town was a summer resort. At the end of March the memsahibs began to arrive, by April they came up in swarms, the road crawling with dandies. You'd have thought there had been a disaster on the plains and these were the stretchers bearing the wounded off to safety. The town, which had been quiet all winter, came alive to the band tunes and voices of Englishwomen.

After the war I was stationed in Bareilly. It was only a day's trip from Debrakot and I took every spare moment in the hills. Latif and I built stables behind the bungalow and I moved a couple of my horses up.

In those days Latif hated me. We never argued but were always on the edge of harsh words. I liked him. He was the best syce I'd ever had and the horses seemed to like him. He had a wife and a daughter. They lived in quarters behind my place in Bareilly but he was not happy there and sometimes complained. Finally I moved him up to Debrakot along with all but one of the horses. Many times I wondered what it was between us. There seemed to be a tension. Was it that I was short-tempered? It was more than that. The hatred seemed to be feeding on his insides like a parasite. His face could not disguise what he felt. Was it my race? Was it my blood? My religion? Latif seemed ready to kill me at any moment. The longer he stayed with me, the more the hatred surfaced, never in words or actions, but in the expression on his face. Even in those days he shaved me and it was with a thrill each morning that I let him put the razor to my face and run it along my throat. He may have felt a thrill as well at the chance to kill me.

A Muslim is a proud man. In his blood there is something which makes him scorn everyone else. He hates with passion. I admired Latif, for in him there was a strength which comes from conviction. That is what made me keep him. Some servants love their employers and fawn over them, boast about them to other servants. The English are flattered by their servants. 'My syce is faithful as a dog,' one told me. I once had a cook who was like that and I fired him as quickly as I could. He was obsequious and I was always worried that I'd trip over him, he was that cringing.

I wanted Latif to hate me. His pride was so strong that I wondered why he shaved me himself and did not let one of the other servants do it. Maybe he enjoyed holding the razor against my throat and tempting his hatred.

He was jealous about the horses and must have whispered things in their ears to make them hate me. But they were only animals, even though their blood was pure, and they were always eager to see me. Latif would stand in the doorway of the stables and watch me go down the line of horses. I would pet each one affectionately, talking to them in English. He spoke to them in Urdu. He would singe his mind with hatred as he watched me. Sometimes he would have to turn and walk away.

I tried to make him hate me even more. It excited me to see him angry, the same feeling I get when watching a horse rear and lash out with its hooves.

Partition, 1947, the English let India slip out of their hands and it broke in two. It was a period of allegiance and hatred. Pride was the emotion of the time and everyone felt kinship to their own race, their own religion, their own families. The politicians were pulled apart, the army was severed, and sides had to be taken.

For us it was a period of confusion; the English abandoned us, not that they had really ever cared who we were or what happened to us. I kept to myself and tried to ignore what was happening. We heard about riots and murders, how trainloads of Muslims on their way to Pakistan were slaughtered and Hindus coming in the other direction were butchered. Every man had to ally himself to one side or the other and there was danger either way. For a while Debrakot remained untouched, but as stories filtered up to the hills about murdered relatives and atrocities in people's home towns, the anger flared up and the first killings took place.

I was sent up to Debrakot along with a detachment of Gurkhas to quell the violence. We set up a camp on the outskirts of town and put the Muslims in there for safety. We curfewed the town for weeks at a time and set up guards on every corner to prevent the looting. I stayed in my own bungalow. Every morning Latif would saddle my horse and I would ride alone through the deserted town. The Gurkhas would salute as I passed them and report incidents. I felt as though I owned the town. I was above its quarrels and jealousies, a firm dictator. These days the town again seems as though it is under curfew. The windows are tightly shut and not a person moves along the streets. As I ride down between the rows of empty shops and collapsing houses, the memory of those days during partition comes back to me. I ride alone. The only sound is that of Elphinstone's hooves slapping the road. They have a crisp echo.

There was a gang in Debrakot during partition which went on a spree of murders. They were young Sikhs, all from good families in town. It was the atmosphere of the times which excited the poison in them. They hunted down an Afghan jewel merchant in the hills around Debrakot where he was hiding. They murdered Ibrahim Hussein in his store and buried him under tins of sardines and pickled onions. They opened his mouth and poured whisky down his throat after they shot him. My Gurkhas tried hard to catch them but they were a clever gang and knew the hills better than anyone.

Often during partition I wished that I was a part of the conflict and not above it. If only I were a Hindu or Muslim or Sikh. If I was an Englishman, at least I could have gone home. Being a half-breed isolated me. I was safe but that was all.

Latif refused to go to the camp. He told me that he and his family would remain in their quarters. There were stories about disease and impropriety in the camps. He was too proud to go and I admired him for it. But I finally made him agree to take a room in our bungalow instead. He wouldn't have done it except for his wife and daughter. They were safer in the big house.

They came for him two days later. Perhaps one of my wife's Hindu servants spread the news that he was still outside the camp. They would have cut Latif's and his wife's and daughter's throats without anyone knowing about it until morning.

I was sitting in our living room, reading the last chapter of a novel. Fortunately it was a dull book and my mind was not completely absorbed. I heard the gate swing open with a high-pitched squeal. Putting the book down slowly, I went over and snuffed out the lamp. In the darkness I crept to the window and looked out. Three young Sikhs with shotguns were slinking along the wall towards Latif's quarters. I had two twelve-bores ready and loaded. Carrying these, I went to Latif's room and woke him. He said nothing but followed me out of one of the back doors of the bungalow. We went quickly to the stables, and as quietly as we could, we saddled my horse.

The three killers had broken into the quarters and we could hear them talking loudly among themselves, their torch beams flickering against the window panes. I told Latif to stay by the door of the stables and cover me. Mounting, I began to urge the horse forward very slowly. For a moment I felt completely exposed and wondered if I would be able to see anything in the darkness. Wouldn't it be better to just ambush the three men and shoot them while they were ransacking the quarters? But it was too late now, I realized. As I drew close to the quarters one of the Sikhs came out of the door.

I held my shotgun steady on him. The other two came out and flashed their torches on me. The light blinded me but I saw a glint off of one of the barrels as the killer aimed at me. I fired right into the torch beam.

There was a startled cry and the torch fell to the ground.

'Be careful,' I said. 'I've another barrel to this gun and one of you will get it before you get me.'

The beams of light hesitated and then moved down to the wounded man, who sat holding his thigh. His young eyes were wide with fear.

'Where is your servant? It's him we want, not you.'

'He's in camp,' I said.

'We'll make sure.'

'No,' I said. 'You'll leave this house alone.'

There was a silent moment. The horse shook his head and pawed at the air. Finally one of the men knelt down and helped his companion onto his shoulder. The other took hold of him from the other side and they began to move slowly out the gate.

'Don't come back unless you want to lick up his blood for him,' I said.

'It will be your blood!'

I fired the second barrel just behind their heels. The three men jumped and then hurried out of the gate. My Gurkhas caught them that night as they were trying to get back to their homes.

I unsaddled the horse myself. Latif was crouching next to the door and did not even seem to notice that I had come in.

'Come on,' I said, grabbing him by the shoulder, 'let's go inside.'

I took him into the living room and sat him down in one of the chairs. First I poured myself a drink. I knew he never touched alcohol. He sat staring at me. I wondered if he was too proud to thank me.

'What made you risk your life?' he finally asked.

I laughed. He didn't. Did he still hate me?

'I'll show you something,' I said, standing up and taking an album off one of the shelves in the bookcase. I leafed through the big volume with its black pages. Finding what I wanted, I passed it over to him. He studied the photograph carefully. It was an old picture of a middle-aged woman, a Muslim, dressed in a satin ghrara with a scarf around her neck. She had moved at the wrong moment, so that her features were a little blurred. She had an air about her, a proud, cruel smile on her lips.

'Your mother?' asked Latif.

I nodded. 'She was a Muslim, the daughter of a musician in Lahore, a dancer. My father married her when he was serving there. He died when I was sixteen and she survived him by ten years. It is of no great consequence. You could never think of me as a Muslim. Look at her, though, and tell me if there is any resemblance.'

'There is,' he said flatly.

I know that she was my mother because I was told that, but I was brought up by an aunt who turned me into what I am. I met my mother once or twice before my father died. She was always very polite to me but never broke into affection. That took a lot of restraint for a Punjabi. I was polite too but I never believed she was my mother until later and I only really felt it that night. It came to me suddenly when they turned those lights on my face. I was exposed. Before that there had been just excitement and fear, but then, there in the yellow glare, I felt an emotion enter me like a thick fluid running through my body. It took a lot to shoot that bastard in the leg rather than the face. It was hatred but it was more than that. I felt as if my mother was there in the house and I was protecting her. I was no longer an Englishman. All of my aunt's lessons, accents, habits – which had been drilled into me – suddenly fell away and I knew who my mother was and I knew why I was facing those men.

3 . *Lost in Action*

The war never ended for me. For a while it died down but now it has flared up again, like an infection. I mean the emotions in me. During the war there was never enough time to think for very long. You never asked who you were because then you wondered why you were there. I fought like anyone else and it was not glorious, even in the end. But while we were fighting our minds were on dying or not dying and nothing else mattered.

In Debrakot the war continues. There is the feeling of being under siege. The houses even look bombed out. The war was an escape for all of us. India was something we forgot, or left behind. We went to North Africa or Burma. It didn't matter where. There has always been a desire in me to rush out of the town, ride down to the foot of the hill, catch a train to the border, and be gone forever. During the war there was a whirlpool in Europe which sucked us all into its madness. Then it spat us out like driftwood, twisted pieces of men.

Lionel has come to stay with us. He is the son of my best friend and is still young enough to have morals, even though he got a

Hindu girl pregnant. He has come up to Debrakot to escape scandal and take over my orchard from me. I am going to retire. It doesn't seem as if it's time for me to retire. My wife keeps bothering me about going to Kenya, where she has relatives. But I wonder what's wrong with Debrakot. It's a safe place for our kind. We've been here now almost thirty years. Our health is fine. Who wants to go to East Africa and get sleeping sickness? But I still feel that urge to run away from India, though I know that I can't. Now that Lionel is here everything seems to be coming to an end. I wish I could feel the excitement again, that I used to have when I married Nat and bought the bungalow and the orchard. Everything used to be full of possibilities and there was a thrill to life. Now there is nothing but monotony. That's what Nat hates. She thinks that leaving Debrakot will solve that. It won't. Our minds are going. We are dying. The first thing to die is our excitement. Our emotions begin to grey. Everything goes a little flat.

The monkeys play hell with my orchard. They come down on the trees in troops of twenty to thirty, break branches, destroy the fruit, holler like children let out of school. Both the rhesus with their red buttocks and the langurs with their black faces and lanky silver bodies descend on my orchard, chasing through the trees, tumbling and frolicking on the ground, fighting, flirting, and screaming.

I used to hire village boys to protect the trees from the time the first blossoms appeared until every apple was picked. But one troop could eat up a year's profit in an afternoon. The boys would get scared or fall asleep and the monkeys, with some secret intuition, would suddenly fall upon the apples like a raiding party. So I came up with the only solution.

I set up a blind at the south end of the ridge, just at the edge of the orchard. That is the direction the langurs usually come from. The rhesus attack from the Debrakot side. Sitting there with my rifle, I can usually hear them coming a few hundred yards away. I wait until they reach the line of oaks opposite the blind. Usually they have their scouts out to recky the area. After a few minutes the entire troop arrives, with the big grey male in command. He is cunning but I have hit him once in the leg. It healed crooked, so that now he walks with a limp.

Our war has been going on for eight months now and the

monkeys have become smarter and smarter. I remember the first time I sat in the blind. That was when I shot the big male in the leg. He came out boldly, expecting nothing worse than a few shouts from the boys and maybe a rock or two thrown at him. He loped forward followed by his lieutenants, four silver males all the same size. Since then I have killed two of them. I waited until he had taken his seat in one of my trees and was chuckling to himself as he watched his harem race into the orchard, the gangly babies scurrying behind their mothers.

The .22 cracked and whined. I heard the smack of the bullet as the leader of the troop leapt backwards off his perch. He ran limping for cover. I fired twice behind him but he was too fast for me. The others were stunned, and then at the scream of one of the lieutenants, they all retreated into the oaks. I shot one young male off the top of an oak where he was watching me. He collapsed and then dropped to the ground with a hollow thud. Monkeys die a lot like men. In fact, their deaths bring them closer to us than anything else about them. The young male was stretched out on the grass, shivering. He held his paw over the wound. I shot him again to finish him off. The rest of the troop vanished down the ridge.

They did not attack again for a month. I hung the dead langur as a warning from one of the trees. He is now a white skeleton, picked clean by the magpies and crows.

The rhesus were more vicious and when I shot the first of their number they did not run like the langurs but came down at me bravely. I was lucky that I had the blind. They encircled me, some on the ground, some in the trees. I held my position and didn't panic but kept firing, two or three shots at a time. I couldn't locate their leader but I killed and wounded eight or nine before they retreated, not with their backs to me like the langurs had done, but with their teeth bared and growling all the time. Those that couldn't walk were carried. I held my fire and let them leave.

They were back the next morning and I could see them from the house when I woke up. It wasn't the fruit they were after. They seemed to be mourning their dead, clustered around each of the bodies, pawing at their lifeless fellows.

There was a mendicant living in the temple at Debrakot. He fed the monkeys every day. When he heard that I was shooting his darlings, he came over to my bungalow and squatted down on the veranda. He said that he would fast until I stopped. Latif and I picked him up and tossed him out. Hindus love animals more than themselves. He lay where we had thrown him for two or three days but then went back to the temple and stopped complaining. He must have become hungry.

Now they come regularly once a month. The langurs are more frightened but they also attack the orchard from time to time, especially when the fruit is on the branches. I wait until I hear them coming and then go down and take up my position. We fight it out for an hour or so. They are smart enough so that they circle me and race into the orchard from all sides. The troop leaders are like generals, giving signals in grunts and screams. As soon as I fire my first shot, they scatter for cover and then begins a game of hide-and-seek. They have learned their cunning from the leopards which hunt them.

Lionel had been with us for a couple of weeks when the monkeys raided the orchard. It was early in the morning and he was still in bed. I woke him up. He didn't seem to understand. I gave him an air rifle and together we sneaked down to the blind. We didn't talk and when he began to ask me what was happening I silenced him with a finger against my lips.

The langurs arrived only a few minutes after us. The two remaining lieutenants sauntered out into the open, with their tails erect and swaying. When they reached the first trees the rest of the troop came bounding out from hiding. 'You take the right-hand one,' I said in a whisper, and aimed. Lionel didn't move.

I had a clear shot, so I fired without waiting. There was a mad rush at the sound of the rifle and not one of the langurs waited around to find out what had happened to the lieutenant. He clutched his stomach and hunched against the trunk of the tree. I killed him with a second shot.

Lionel looked at me, surprised. I tried to smile. He was shocked that I had killed the langur.

'They damage the fruit,' I said.

He began to stand up and leave.

'If I didn't kill them they'd come back for more. I don't grow the fruit for their feasting, damn it.'

He had an accusing look in his eye. But he said nothing.

As he walked up the hill, I shouted: 'Do you feel sorry for them? Are you a bloody Hindu? Are these your goddamned holy monkeys?'

The war still goes on.

4 . *Pedigree*

I wonder if he remembers. Those eyes still haunt me, wide and curious under the curtain in the doorway where he was hiding, watching our drunken games and arguments. Does he remember that night, the way I remember it, through his eyes? I noticed his presence just as Millie started dragging me off to her room and Charles followed Nat to bed. Lionel couldn't have been more than three. I can't remember anything from when I was three. But I remember his eyes. They clung to me and seemed to be all about us in the darkness of Millie's room. He seemed to be there in the room listening, hearing every sigh and moan, watching us. If he doesn't remember, at least I do, which is twice as bad.

We were in their house in Lucknow. It was late and all four of us had been drinking. Nat and I had come down from Debrakot for a visit. We had always been close, inseparable. Charles, Teddy, Millie, and Nat. If only marriages consisted of four instead of two. Our names went together like four notes in a measure. Four hands at bridge, a foursome at golf, a table for four.

The room was that late-night yellow, subdued. The air had a thick smell of rum. We were all hazy-eyed and thick-tongued, so that we spoke softly and with a lisp. It had been two and a half years since we'd been together. Lionel had been born at our house in Debrakot. For some strange reason his birth broke us apart. But that night we were together again. Lionel was asleep in his room, or at least we thought he was.

Charles was telling hunting stories. He began talking in a low voice which gradually increased in volume, until we suddenly noticed that he was shouting. He went into his room and brought out his twelve-bore. Loading it, he aimed and fired at a bison head on the wall. The trophy exploded into a dozen pieces of dry skin and clay. I took the gun away from him and made Millie pick up a stuffed pheasant from the mantelpiece. She threw it as far away from her as she could. I blasted it twice in the air and it dropped onto the coffee table amidst a blizzard of feathers.

Charles and I had an argument after he had shot the leopard on the sofa and blasted four panes of glass out of the roshandans. I forget what we were fighting about. Maybe it was Lionel. The women broke us apart. Millie grabbed me and Nat took hold of Charles. It happened naturally. My wife went with Charles and I with Millie. Just then I saw Lionel. Maybe the shots had woken him up, or Charles's shouting. He was lying on the brick floor hidden partly by the sill, peering under the curtain like a mouse inside its hole. There was no fear in his eyes, only a childish understanding. I thought, my God, does he know what's happening? I felt not guilty but afraid, afraid that he would remember.

Whenever the four of us had been together, we had often traded off. It wasn't a crass sort of arrangement. These weren't orgies. The four of us were close and it didn't seem at all wicked. But that changed when Lionel was born. Whom did he belong to? He was Millie's baby but who was the father?

There had been so many nights that it was hard to tell. Of course, Charles took Lionel because Millie was his wife. But could it have been the night Millie and I were up on the roof in the Barsati? That was the night the mosquitoes attacked us, hundreds of them, swarms, whining about us like a bomber raid. I lay on top of Millie to protect her because there were no sheets to cover us and got bitten all over my back. It itched for two days whenever I sat down.

He looks a little like Charles, but that could be just chance. It might have been the night Millie told me she wished Charles made love like I did. God knows, we never thought it would happen, even though we talked about it.

Nat never got pregnant, neither by me nor by Charles. She's like a dry well. No matter how many times you put the bucket in, nothing comes out.

When Nat and I heard about Millie getting pregnant, it was as if we had already known about it. I wanted a child. Even a girl would have been all right. But Nat wouldn't give me one. Perhaps Lionel was my son and Charles stole him from me. It was the same as knocking a cricket ball for six into the neighbours' yard and then having the neighbours' son steal the ball.

Now that Lionel is here in Debrakot, I keep wondering if he is my son or not. I watch him when he isn't looking and wait for his genes to betray him. He is soft-spoken. Maybe Charles beat him when he was a child and that has made him sullen. God, I'll kill Charles if he's made my son into a tulip. The look on his face when I shot that langur. It was the same look he had when he was lying in the doorway. He was not surprised, only very aware of what was happening. It was as if what he had seen when he was three made him understand everything from then on. They say an incident opens a man's eyes. Perhaps what he saw – his mother and me – he did not understand at the time. Perhaps he doesn't remember it now, but what he saw is imprinted on his mind and it twists his understanding, like a flaw in a pane of glass.

Charles brought Millie up to Debrakot to have Lionel. He was in the middle of a lot of work and had to go right back down to Lucknow. He only stayed for a night. Millie was tired and went to bed early. Nat lay around for a while on the sofa and then she went in to her room to sleep. Charles and I played cards most of the night.

Charles plays very seriously and hates to lose. He drinks a lot when he plays and says it helps his concentration, but I know that when he's had too much he begins to lose quickly and gets mad.

We began playing with chips and then switched to coins after an hour or so. In a while there were notes on the table as well. Charles liked to play high. I am not a gambler and it gives me no thrill to put my money down. Never having really lost or won, I suppose I don't know what it feels like. The level in the bottle dropped as we played, until the cards seemed to float in and out of our hands, hopping onto the table of their own accord. Neither of us was winning. Then suddenly my mind cleared and I felt immediately sober. I began to play precisely and with great care. Charles was sloppy and so drunk I had to shuffle for him, because when he tried he dropped the pack on the floor. I began to win. The money piled up higher in front of me. I played seriously and with a calculating desperation, as if everything depended on this game. Charles was losing his temper and shouted at me when I tried to hurry him.

Usually if cards become too hot, I stop playing and say I have to go to bed, but that night the more serious the game grew, the more compulsive I became. A strange idea came into my mind. I would beat Charles. I would empty his wallet, win the clothes off his back, defeat him in every way I could. And, instead of a pound of flesh, I would make him gamble away the child in Millie's stomach. His eyes were yellow and squinted at me across the table. Perhaps he sensed my desperation but he could not stop himself. He knew what we were playing for, not the chips, the coins, or the bills. It was the baby. He knew I was going to win in the end, but he played on like a man who knows he is finished. The stakes were as high as they could get. The money seemed to be insignificant and the coins fell on the table with an annoying clatter, like women's voices, small talk. Neither of us needed to acknowledge the stakes and when Charles's money ran out we played another hand. He won a couple of the bills back and then lost them again. Both of us said nothing. Charles stared hard at me while I arranged my hand. Why didn't he quit?

The bottle was empty and so were our glasses. I was still sober. The excitement had flushed me. It seemed as if everything I had lived for lay on the blank surface of the table. Earlier that night when Millie had gone to bed, I went in to say good night to her. She was lying on her back with her belly humped up in front of her. Her hands were stroking Lionel's tiny head through the wall of her abdomen. She took my hand and put it against her. It was like feeling a present before you open it to guess what is inside.

Charles knew it was the last hand and I dealt it out carefully, snapping each of the cards down onto the table with finality. I knew I had won. Charles shuddered when he picked his cards up and refused to play the hand out. He said he was sleepy and staggered to his feet. His hunched form swayed through the door. I swept the cards into a pile, resisting the urge to have a look at his hand. My own I left face down as well. There was no need to see them. The verdict was inevitable. The money meant nothing to me and I divided it in half and put my share in my pocket. Charles was asleep with his clothes on when I went into the room. Millie lay in the bed beside him, her mouth open and her eyes turned back under her lids. They were both snoring softly. I found Charles's trousers and put the money in his wallet. Before going back to my room I ran my hands very gently over Millie.

A frightening sensation ran through me as my fingers caressed her belly. It made me recoil. I wanted to tear her open, peel away the skin, have the child immediately. I could see myself pulling him out of her, leaving her hollow. I would have him now and carry him to my own bed. He would be mine from then on. I took my hands away from her and turned to leave. It would kill her, I thought. But that didn't matter to me. If only I could have the child. Millie woke and mumbled something in a drowsy voice. I left quietly, the sweat breaking out on my forehead.

THREE . *Peacocks*

The shuttlecock rose gracefully over the net like a leaping dolphin and then pitched down at me in a smooth curve. I am always clumsy, especially when I'm drunk. My arm swung the racket underneath it, trying to be accurate. I listened for the taut 'ping'. There was no sound. My arm swept lazily up and across my body, the racket looking more like a rajah's fan than a battledore. Somebody chuckled. I looked back and tried to force a smile but the men were all playing cards and the ladies were talking. The shuttlecock lay on the ground like a discarded petticoat. I thought I caught Stephanie's eye but then I realized it had been a man's laugh.

'Come on, Nat, your serve!' screeched Angela. She was just showing off, proving that she is better than me. I leaned over and picked the shuttlecock off the ground as if it were a dead bird. Giving myself a moment's rest, I let the birdie drop and then slapped it across. I knew it hit the frame but at least it went over the net. Angela made an awkward lunge, as if this were a championship match. She is so damned competitive.

'You shouldn't give such difficult serves, Nat,' she said. 'We're only having fun. Why not try to get a rally going?' I didn't say anything. I don't like to talk when I'm drunk, even on a picnic, because I know that once I start talking, I won't stop. The birdie came at me again, this time like a hawk. It hovered above me in the air a moment and then dropped. But I hit it. I hit it as hard as I could. Angela stepped back and tripped. She fell right on her wide ass. She was as drunk as I. Again I heard the laughter. The men were still playing cards and ignoring us. Maybe it was a faun or a satyr hidden in the bushes, watching our picnic with amusement.

We have always had fine picnics in Debrakot, long-drawn-out affairs, starting at half past ten in the morning and carrying on until dusk. One person makes sandwiches and chips, another salad, a third brings dessert, and those who want bring their bottled beer and some bring whisky.

It used to be an opportunity for young people to fall in love and old people to talk about it. There are always cards for the men and gossip for the ladies. When there were youngsters in Debrakot, they played badminton and went for surreptitious little treks out of sight. Those women with daughters were always nervous, while those who had boys swore they were honourable. If I'd had a daughter, I'd have worried about other people's sons. As a girl I was worse than any boy. I would take them behind the house and make them pull their pants down, to see what they were hiding. I made them kiss me on the lips when I was ten and enjoyed being tickled. I goosed one of my playmates so hard that his mother wouldn't let us play together any more. I think I even dreamt that Father Christmas came up my chimney.

Stephanie brought some of the wine her sister makes. The men had whisky, so we finished off three bottles between the six of us. It was strong wine and actually Jessica only had a little. Padre Joseph and his wife sat on the bench and watched us get drunk. He is the pastor of our church and is from Kerala. His wife is as black as a Negro and they always smell of coconut oil. We have to invite them even though he doesn't play cards and she doesn't drink. We have to invite him to say grace. As a concession, we let him say it twice, once before lunch and once before tea. He drags it out as long as his English lasts. He manages to stretch his vocabulary over ten minutes sometimes. It's one of those situations where you wish whoever it was that invited them the first time hadn't, but now that it's become a tradition you have to.

The picnics aren't so much fun any more. There should be youngsters – they have all gone to Mussoorie or Simla for school or to Delhi for work. We gather without them and pretend we're happy. We all drink a little more than we used to.

I could hear the four of them talking about me. The words were muffled but it didn't matter, because I know what they say, because I've spent the last twenty-five years talking with them.

– Poor Nat, she's drunk again.

– It's too bad when a person needs to get drunk.

– Especially since that boy's visiting.

– I wonder what he thinks.

– It's embarrassing.

– Poor Nat, she should have had children.

– Yes, they would have been good for her.

Angela served again. This time I returned it with some poise, no tripping or wild smashes into the net. She hit it again, very high, so there was plenty of time to judge it. I was off balance. I knew it before I swung. My whole body seemed to follow the shot as if the shuttlecock were a magnet pulling me towards it. I felt as if I was filled with air, my head especially. My feet left the ground. When I fell it was as if I had landed on a thick mattress. The wind was knocked out of me. Everything felt fuzzy. I am too drunk to be playing badminton, I said to myself. I heard him laughing again, whoever he was. I lay on the grass a moment. Angela was laughing too, but her laugh is high and shrill. This laugh I didn't recognize. I raised my head and looked around. The racket and shuttlecock were lying where they had fallen in front of me. I scanned the group. They were all looking at me. Teddy looked angry. The others were smiling and laughing. Picnics are always jolly.

Suddenly I found him. I had almost forgotten he was there, sitting with his back against one of the chestnut trees. He was not chuckling any more but I could see the smile on his young face. He was grinning like a jackal.

He was laughing at all of us. He was laughing at us for our old ways, our old clothes, our games, our silly picnics, and our drunkenness. He was probably wishing there were young girls to take into the bushes and rape, one by one. If I were still his age, I would have shown him. I would have taken him into the bushes instead. He escaped, just like any man does. He could run away from that Hindu girl and come up here to us, out of anyone's reach. He is safe, to lean against the trunk of that chestnut, staring off at the mountains, while that girl is lying on her back somewhere, watching her belly rise like a mountain. Young men have always been able to run away.

I was very beautiful when I was young. You wouldn't guess it by looking at me now. The most beautiful women always grow ugliest with age. That's because their beauty is fragile. I love those few moments just after it rains, when the leaves are delicate with drops of water and if you touch anything it explodes into a shower. Everything is perfect for a moment and the beauty lies in its uncertainty. You don't know whether it's going to pour again or whether the sun will intrude and dry everything to dust. Whatever happens, those few moments just after it rains are the most tenuous and beautiful. After I had been beautiful, my face began to wither quickly and then it cracked like old porcelain. I got too thin and the tendons showed on my hands. My eyes grew too sharp, until they were cruel. My tits began to sag. No man would keep me when I was beautiful because they sensed my fragility, they knew I would get old before them, that my skin would turn dark and leathery. It was just like people not wanting to buy silver any more because it tarnishes so quickly. I had to wait until I was ugly again, as ugly as when I was a baby. Finally Teddy came along and I guess he was desperate, like any soldier is after the fighting stops.

Daddy was a canal inspector. We had a house in Allahabad, where I lived when Mother was alive. When she died it was too lonely a place to keep and Daddy sold it. I was at school then, so I didn't need a home except on holidays. Daddy was on tour most of the time and when he wasn't he lived with my uncle in Agra. Most of my holidays were spent in inspection bungalows along the canals. I went to a convent in Delhi. Daddy would pick me up at the beginning of the holidays and I would join him on tour. I saw a lot of places and got to know the canals, their whisper echoing the roar of the great rivers they came from. I learned their geography, how they ran like a network of veins in a man's hand, flowing into each muscle and sinew, giving life and energy to each finger. I always pictured India as a huge hand with the canals flowing into it.

About thirty miles from Fatehgarh there is a small canal, lined with babbul and mango trees. It was during the winter and the newly planted wheat was shooting up in a bristly green. Daddy had an old Austin which was so low to the ground that it scraped every few minutes. Daddy and I rode in the back with scarves around our faces because of the dust. There was an old cook there whom Daddy called 'Tom'. He was as black as a drain, but he cooked good food and kept a wonderful garden. He had put in flower beds around the whole bungalow and edged them with bricks. The front was a jungle of marigolds, each one like a bright, bulbous sun. He had a bouquet of them on the table when we came in. Each pillar of the veranda was shrouded in a clambering purple bougainvillaea. In the gardens at the back of the house and along the side there were larger plants, bird of paradise and hollyhocks.

'Tom', whose real name was Din Mohammed, killed one of the chickens running around the yard and made us a curry that night. Afterwards Daddy and I sat on the porch and listened to the muted noises of the plains, the soft pulse of the canal, the peacocks in the mango trees, the throbbing snicker of the grist mill. I remember wondering what it was like for Daddy to be alone so much of the time.

Daddy was always alone. He was very careful of who he was and because of that he kept aloof from those below him. Those above him kept themselves aloof. Watching him that evening, I wanted to tell him, when I was a little girl and Mother would take me on trips to the hills, we would stop at a canal to picnic on the way and I would point at the water and say, 'That's Daddy's canal.' I never thought there was anyone above him. I never did.

The third night we were there, Tom was serving us dinner. There was a knock at the door and it opened. The light from the kerosene lanterns made it look as if you were peering through amber. A tall figure, perfectly erect, stepped inside. He was an Englishman, a policeman; his helmet was held in the crook of his arm and I caught in his eye a tinge of insolence when he looked at Daddy. It disappeared as soon as he turned his head towards me. We stared at each other in surprise. His straw-blonde hair was plastered down on his forehead from wearing the helmet. He had a narrow moustache and his chin jutted out forcefully.

'How do you do?' He put his hand out to Daddy. 'Kenneth Thatcher, Deputy Superintendent of Police, Etah.'

A little flustered, Daddy introduced himself and me.

'I'm afraid I had a bit of bad luck. My men and I were out after the dakoos. Our car broke down about a mile from here; the axle snapped in two just like a piece of sugarcane. We were hoping to get to Etah tonight but I guess we'll have to wait until morning. These damned cunker roads! They should be offbounds for oxcarts. That's what ruins them.'

'Have a seat,' said Daddy. 'There's plenty of food too.'

'No, it's quite all right. I didn't realize you were here, otherwise I wouldn't have bothered you. I was just going to spend the night and push off in the morning.'

He was flattering us and Daddy was easy prey. He stood up, took the policeman by the arm, and with an awkward gesture of welcome pushed him into the chair across from me.

'I really don't . . .' began the Englishman, then he looked at me and hesitated. 'Well, I suppose I am hungry.'

'Of course you are,' said Daddy.

Tom brought in some hot curry and a steaming plate of pulao. Kenneth Thatcher helped himself generously. Daddy and I watched him, like birds watching a cobra. He had impressed us with his manners. We were not used to being treated with such civility by an Englishman. We were victims of our own pride. He was sloppy at eating and smacked his lips. It didn't matter to us. Daddy didn't even wince when he told Tom to bring him some sliced onions. We just grinned like apes.

I was eighteen and my face still got hot every time I saw a man. All during dinner I watched Kenneth Thatcher with the rice dribbling down his handsome chin and the yellow curry stains around his lips. He spoke with Daddy about dacoits. He told stories about chasing the bandits through sugarcane fields, where you couldn't see more than a foot ahead of you. We heard about the capture of Talwar Singh two years before, which had made the Delhi papers. He had been involved and was actually the man who caught Talwar Singh after the dacoit escaped the first time. Daddy said that he thought he remembered his name from the papers. Daddy was thirty years older than the Englishman and yet he was running happy circles around him like an eager puppy. The DSP would look at me and smile kindly, not letting on that he was having a joke at our expense.

After dinner we moved to the veranda and Daddy produced a bottle of scotch from his suitcase. He didn't usually drink, except on special occasions and then he always drank too much.

'It's nice to get stranded out here in the middle of nowhere and find people with sensitivities and taste. You know, I get tired of being a policeman; all the time you're dealing with the scum of the population – a rotten, distasteful lot of people. It's not good for a man. It makes you callous and crude.'

'Well, I wish we had more to offer you,' said Daddy.

'No, no, you've given me more than I deserve. I'm honoured.'

Daddy was drinking too quickly. He was nervous. I could tell by the way he giggled at the end of every phrase. The DSP was cold sober. He remained polite, and when Daddy's head finally fell forward onto his chest, he helped me carry him into the bedroom and put him to bed.

'Shall we take a walk before turning in?' said the policeman. 'It's a perfect night.'

I wanted to say no. I thought about Daddy, lying there unconscious in the next room. Tom had locked the back door and gone to sleep. It was one of those moments when the wind stops blowing and the grass is still. I wanted to say yes.

I said, 'All right. Just a short walk, though, I'm tired.'

He smiled at me as he held the door open. We stood a moment at the edge of the veranda. There was no moon. It was one of those moments which you want to inhale, to completely absorb and never forget. You want the memory of it to gyrate in your mind, like a top which only needs to be spun once and it spins forever. Sometimes your memory twirls so fast that it disappears and at other times it slows down and begins to wobble, as if it is going to stop. He jumped down off the veranda and held a hand out to me. I didn't take it. I jumped without his help.

'It's lonely out here, isn't it?' he said.

'Yes, Mr Thatcher.'

'Oh Gawd, don't call me that. There can't be five years between us, Natalie. Call me Kenneth. Only my men call me Mr Thatcher.' His arm swung confidently around my shoulder and I felt the way a fawn must feel when a python wraps its first coil around it. But that's what I think now, now that I'm old and wrinkled. At that time it was different. I knew there was something wrong and the onions on his breath smelled like poison, but he was English and handsome. We turned away from the road and followed the canal. I could not see the water, it was so dark. My feet followed each other, like suspicious men. A few stars were visible through the dust haze. I was on his right side.

'The pistol's a nuisance,' he said. 'Why don't you come over to my left.' His one arm passed me across to the other. It was an automatic gesture. I felt as if I were being handed from one man to another. I was helpless, like a piece of luggage.

We walked on without saying anything. After a while, I could feel his nervousness and it comforted me. He pulled me tight against his side, crushing my arm between us. His fingers, clenched over my shoulder, were sweating. I wanted to laugh. He was afraid of me, afraid of how young I was. I could hear it in his breathing. It was like asthma. I thought about the stories he had told us and wanted to ask him if he felt like this when he chased dacoits. Suddenly I wasn't weak any more, struggling in his grip. I was queen.

The night wasn't frightening any more. The canal had a reassuring sound and every time the peacocks rustled in the mango trees I smiled because I knew they were watching me and laughing too. My feet stepped lightly now. I wanted to dance on top of him. I wanted to grind him into the dust. I wanted to leave him there writhing on the ground like a snake with its back broken. His muscles shivered against me. He probably wished he'd drunk more to build up his courage. I was scared too. Scared of myself perhaps, of what I could do to him. He could do anything to me but it wouldn't make any difference. I would still be dancing on top of him, still a queen.

I reached around his waist. His back was wide and strong. The coarse cloth of his khaki uniform felt scaly. As my arm went around him, he pulled me close again. I could feel his relief. His whole body seemed to sigh. I stifled a giggle and wondered what would happen if I took my arm away.

The canal is lined with trees – shesham, babbul, neem, and mango, especially mango. Their roots are sunk deep in the moist soil, retrieving what seeps out of the current into the earth. They stand like sentinels guarding the water. At night, their leaves lapping the air, they transmit the whispered secret of what the shepherdess dreamt when she sat in their shade as her cows drank at the canal. Her dreams creep out of the foliage at night and dance with the blue god. The trees hide their revelry and stand guard over the dreams when they fall exhausted and silent to the ground.

'Are you still in school?' he asked.

I lied. 'No, I'm not. Do I look like a schoolgirl?'

'Of course not.' He chuckled. I wanted to chuckle back at him, but my voice wasn't gruff enough and it came out as a giggle.

'Are you scared?' he asked.

'No,' I said. 'Why should I be when the Deputy Superintendent has an arm around me and a pistol on his hip?' If the sisters at the convent had heard me say that, I would have been on restriction for a year. I felt wicked and lovely.

'Have you got any boy friends?' he asked.

'A few,' I said.

'Give me their names and addresses and I'll send my men to arrest them, just to have you to myself,' he said with a quavering laugh.

'They'd probably run away when they saw you coming. You know, you're such a frightening fellow.' I don't know whether I actually said any of this or whether it's what I added on later when I told my friends the story after 'lights out' in the dormitory. We used to read a lot of romance novels on the sly and I probably took the dialogue from one of them. It could be me talking now, though, putting a middle-aged imagination into my teen-aged mouth. Anyway, we talked, and what we said isn't what's important. What I imagined is.

I tried to imagine the peacocks roosting above us. That afternoon I had watched them feeding in the fields on the other side of the canal. There had been four flocks, each with two or three gaudy males and a harem of brown hens. As the sun set over the canal, burnishing everything in its demise, each flock in turn took to the air, their heavy wings beating painfully as they fought to keep aloft and then glided into the trees along our bank. Their mournful calls, like clarinets, echoed down the ribbon of water, relayed from flock to flock, until finally the darkness silenced them. I have always wanted to have a garden full of tame peacocks, so that in the evening I could listen to them calling.

He was getting even more nervous. I could feel him sweating through his shirt. When he spoke it was only in short sentences. He kept glancing down at me. I leaned my head against his shoulder for a second.

'Are you married?' I asked.

His laugh blurted out like a rifle shot. 'No, don't worry about that,' he said. 'I have no commitments.'

I put my head down again. This time he kissed my forehead, gently. We stopped walking. There was a mango tree above us and I was looking up into its branches, trying to find a peacock, when both his arms came around me like jaws and he seemed to swallow me with a kiss. I was surprised and awkward. My long hair had come between us and I could feel it in my mouth. He pulled his head back and brushed the strands away. We kissed again. His mouth was harsh. His tongue was rough like a cat's. I thought of Daddy. I tried to dance but my feet wouldn't move. I wanted to grind my heel into his spine and paralyse him, but he had me caught too tightly in his arms. I wanted to fight. I wanted to yell. I wanted to send him slithering away into the bushes. We fell. I knew I was no longer queen. I felt his nervousness spill out of him and something flow in to replace it. I felt his anger. I felt his bitterness. I wanted to laugh but I was crying.

When it was over, the first thing I remember is hearing the peacocks moving above us.

'Do you have a torch?' he asked. His voice was as it had been at the dinner table when he was talking with Daddy.

I didn't understand. 'Do you have a torch?' he asked again.

'Back at the bungalow. In my suitcase.'

'Stay here a minute,' he said. I felt him get off me. I felt as if I had been cut in two, like an apple. I heard him fastening his belt. His footsteps walked away.

Lying there in the blank darkness, I listened to the gentle sounds of the canal as it flowed south, moving as silently as a snake through dust. I smiled to myself. The tree loomed above me and for a moment it was so quiet that I thought I heard the slow sucking of its roots, like serpents stealing milk from the raw nipples of a young mother.

The torch flickered from the veranda and then I heard him coming towards me through the darkness.

'Why don't you get up?' he said, offering me a hand.

He pulled me to his side and kissed me on the cheek abruptly, without any gentleness, like a parakeet when you hold it up to your face and it pecks at you.

'Watch this,' he said.

The torch beam flashed into the mango tree, illuminating its leafy branches with an eerie yellow. It danced from spot to spot until suddenly it stopped. A peacock turned sideways in the glare, the light glistening off its feathers, its long serpentine neck arched in surprise. The pistol had a dull, flat report. I heard a thud, as the bird hit the ground. Kenneth turned his head towards me and smiled. In the yellow light his face was the colour of old wax. He grinned like a jackal.

'You can have it for dinner tomorrow night,' he said.

I didn't get pregnant. My friends told me I was lucky. They said I should have screamed or kicked him but I know they were just jealous. It was a few years later when I realized that I didn't have to worry. I couldn't have a child even if I wanted one. I never told anybody. I enjoyed watching men get worried afterwards and make me promise to write them if anything happened. I always made them feel as if they'd raped me. One sailor I met in Bombay wrote me a letter from every port he landed at, asking about his child. He really expected one and would have come back and married me if I'd had it. Finally I wrote to him and told him nothing had happened. He never answered. Maybe the next girl, in the next port, had got pregnant. I didn't even have that trap, if I'd wanted it. I couldn't scare anyone into marrying me. At least nobody left me holding the bag.

I have always been left, though.

I decided I wouldn't play badminton any more, after I fell. I was too drunk to do anything but drink. Lionel wasn't watching me now. He was staring up into the chestnut trees. Padre Joseph and his wife came over and said goodbye. We watched them waddle off.

'It's too bad there's no company for poor Lionel,' said Jessica.

'He looks so lonely,' said Angela.

'He's probably mooning over that girl of his; she was a Hindu, wasn't she, Nat?'

I didn't answer. I didn't want to talk. I stood up unsteadily and walked over to where the men were playing cards. Mr Saunders had his back against the ice box. He didn't even look at me, he was so absorbed in his game. I lifted the lid and took out the bottle of gin Teddy had brought. There was a bottle of lemonade also. Teddy eyed me over his hand. Except for his moustache, he looked like a geisha girl peering over her fan. Only Angela joined me in a drink. The others are scared of their husbands. Angela would be too, if hers were alive.

Picnics were always for the children. We should stop having them now that they've left. We could just as well sit at home and the men could have one room to play cards in and we could all sit in another and get drunk and talk about whoever isn't there. Every month they trudge up here like a little band of pilgrims, remembering what it was like carrying their children up in their arms or nervously watching them scamper ahead always too close to the edge and not looking. They sit and talk about the time Jessica's Ann fell out of the chestnut tree and got a concussion – she is married now, to a man in advertising – or the time Angela's nephew came up from Calcutta and discovered a rat snake coiled up under a rock – he has emigrated to Australia. I have no children to remember. The others come up here to find theirs, expecting them to appear out of the bushes and run towards us, a squealing throng, all dressed in white and carrying badminton rackets in their hands. They used to run to their mothers and fathers, clambering for kisses and jumping up to be hugged. It would be like meeting a ship. Teddy would stand up, place his cards face down, and very slowly walk over to me. We would stand beside each other and watch the reunion in silence. Now I can laugh at them because their children are gone. They only have their memories and our ritual picnics. Their children will never come running out of the bushes again.

One Easter we had a picnic and everyone wore white. That year there were lots of children in Debrakot and I remember they had four games of badminton going at the same time. The shuttlecocks bounced back and forth, in time with the fluttering heartbeats of the young girls. They squealed and ran in silly circles while the boys, hands on their hips, made it all look so easy. It was like a dream in which everyone is young, the shuttlecocks arching through it like hopes. There was a huge cake frosted with marzipan and cream puffs, mints, and lots of gin. In those days the skirts were full, with plenty of crepe bows and chiffon scarves, which were only meant for the wind to catch and blow. In those skirts you always walked as if it were windy, even if it wasn't. The men looked as if they were dressed for a cricket match. Jessica's father was alive then and I remember him, sitting on the bench, wearing a suit as white as his goatee. He had a white golfing hat on too, and whenever any one of us passed, he would try to whistle and wink. He was so cute, sort of on a last fling.

They hate Lionel because when they see him they realize that their children aren't children any more. For the first time I have a son but he's already grown up.

The chestnuts are in bloom. Their flowers have a strange smell, like perfume the morning after a party. Two of the trees stand at the bottom of the ridge, overshadowing a stone bench. From there you can see Debrakot, its rusty tin roofs spattered across the hill. None of the roofs have been painted for years. The whole town is going to rust away, like a broken tricycle left in the long grass at the back of the yard, a relic of childhood. Some day it will disappear and all that will be left of it will be a red dust, powdering the ridge. No one will look back. We will all be buried here and our bones will disintegrate like the town. A hundred years from now, farmers will come and see the red colour of this earth and think it fertile. They will try to raise crops which will never sprout. Their children will catch sickness from the earth and in the end it will be left again, desolate and forgotten.

Those chestnuts were planted by Colonel Robin Smellie, who was the first man to settle in Debrakot. He also built the bench, placed where the sun first hits in the morning, where it is hottest at noon, and where it makes its final departure like an ascending prophet. The chestnuts have grown, though, and now the bench is perpetually in shade. On up the ridge there are the scattered ruins of a shooting lodge, also built by Colonel Smellie. We always use the spot for our picnics. He was a soldier in the Company's service. When he was not leading charges against Pindaris and Gurkhas or tying black men across a cannon's orifice and blasting the treachery out of them, Smellie enjoyed the quiet pleasures of hunting among the dimpled hills, where he chased muntjaks and sambur through the rippled shadows as eagerly as if they had been stags in the Scottish Highlands.

*

During the war I was in Calcutta. I had a secretarial job with the government and rented an apartment with two other girls. We would go out together at night and meet soldiers in the smoky bars of the decrepit city. Alice, one of my friends, finally met a New Zealander who married her and took her home with him after the war was over. I never kept to anyone in particular. Because I hated them, I never wanted to know who they were and what they'd done. It would always upset me when they lay beside me and talked about home in Ireland, where it was always green because of the mists, not like India, and the houses were far apart. The ocean was always cold and Prussian blue – white where it pounded against the cliffs – not brown and slow like the Hoogly. I wanted to throw them off their green Irish cliffs into the ocean and hear them squeal as they hit the cold waves. I wanted to tell them that I used to dream of green hills and blue oceans. I wanted to say I was tired of the dusty tan of this country. I wanted to cry like an exile and ask to be taken home but I knew I couldn't because I was home. I was shipwrecked on my own shore but I didn't realize it. I kept looking down the Hoogly and thinking that if only I could catch the right current it would take me home.

I got to hate men. I hated their smell, the sound of their breathing, and listening to them talk. I was losing my prettiness, though. I was wilting, and even when I hated them the most, I needed men more than anything else. It was like hating myself. I dug my fingernails into their backs and bit them like an angry pet. They thought it was love that unsheathed my claws and that my teeth were as innocent as a playful kitten's.

In 'forty-two the Americans came. The Japanese had reached Burma. Manila and Singapore had fallen. Everyone was scared, especially the Bengalis. They were parasites whose foster tree was going to be cut out from under them. There was talk of revolution and welcoming the Japanese. The Americans didn't understand any of it. They worked on their airplanes all day and drank most of the night. We swapped them bottles of cheap whisky for their beer.

The American GIs were simple. They were scared too, just like the rest of us, but they didn't understand the English or the Bengalis. They wanted a good time, just in case it was their last. For them it was only the Japs against the rest of us. I liked them better than the English. The English knew our secrets and they hated us for it. The Americans had no idea who we were. 'By your accent I'd swear to God you were English. But I've been there and the girls in London weren't like you.' The Americans liked us. They figured we weren't as likely to give them syphilis as the Bengalis. I hadn't lost my beauty by then, either. The war was a good time for us because nobody had a moment to stop and think about who we were. Drinks went down quicker and there were more of them. You didn't have to talk too much. Even the English loosened up. Calcutta was a big enough city so that you never met the same guy twice.

One day Alice and Patty and I brought home three American pilots. This was before Alice had met the fellow from New Zealand that took her home with him. The airmen were already drunk off their feet by the time we got them into our apartment. I took a captain from Iowa. He was younger than I and so drunk that every time he lay down he'd get dizzy and start to retch. Finally he fell asleep, curled up between me and the wall.

I remember lying in my room, listening to Alice and another captain from Utah, who said he was a Mormon. The captain from Iowa talked in his sleep but I couldn't understand what he was saying. The only Americans I'd met before had been missionaries. Suddenly I thought I wanted to go to America. At least I would be away from the English. A feeling in my navel wound up and burrowed through me like an auger, tearing me apart. Each twist drilled my hatred through me. I was lonely. Daddy had been killed in a car accident near Nainital but that was five years before. I wanted to shake the pilot from Iowa by the shoulder and wake him up and tell him to take me back with him to America. I could see myself wandering through New York, Los Angeles, or Chicago. They would think I was Spanish. It would be home. I would have caught the right current and sailed into New York. The huge buildings would close in and protect me. People would stop me and ask, 'Are you Spanish?' and I would say, 'No, I'm his wife,' and point to the flyer from Iowa, whose hair would have grown long enough to part, now that he was out of the air force. He was the only man, except for Teddy, that I ever told the truth to.

'You sure you can't have a kid?' he asked.

'Yeah, you'll take me back. Like a trophy, you'll take me back, packed alongside a Jap sword, a gold medallion with Hirohito's picture on it, and whatever you scrounge off the battlefield when the fighting stops. I'll mean as much to you as a tooth pulled out of some bastard you shot.' I don't know why I said any of it. I really didn't hate him.

'Hey, what's gotten into you?'

'You're all full of crap,' I said. Alice and I used to practise talking like Americans.

'Come on, what about last night?'

'I lied to you about last night. It wasn't great. It was awful. You were so drunk you couldn't do anything. I stared at your back all night.'

'Hey, wait a minute,' he said. 'What about your omelette?'

'Eat it yourself,' I said, and walked out.

He wouldn't have taken me to America. I wonder if he even made it back over the hump, the poor American from Iowa.

Teddy was losing. I could tell by the way he was staring at his cards. All the men ever do in Debrakot is play cards or chess, from morning till late into the night. They were all lounging on the ground with their Gurkha hats on, looking like Greta Garbos and Rita Hayworths. It's decadent. They're bored. I went over and leaned on Teddy's shoulder. He had two queens. He put them down. It looked like it was his trick. Mr Saunders was smoking a cigar; he put down a pair of kings.

'That's not fair,' I said as he picked up the cards and shuffled.

'Shut up, Nat,' said Teddy. 'You're drunk. Go lie down and sleep it off.'

'In chess ...' I started to say, but the men weren't listening to me. Teddy was scowling. The hand he'd just been dealt was awful.

I went back over and joined the ladies again. They were talking as they always do, about their children. I watched them carefully. Each one of them retained a faint suggestion of her youth, enough details so that you could have recognized an early photograph taken of her when she was twenty. Behind each of the ash-grey faces was a little fire, smouldering in withered cheeks. They must still put on lace negligés, I thought, and try to get a rise out of their husbands. Teddy and I quit long ago. Now I put down a couple of drinks before I go to bed and forget about it, even though sometimes I want to go back to Calcutta and live it all over again for the excitement. I'm scared to go back to that city now; most of the old bars will be closed. There will be plenty of drunk businessmen and a few refugee poets but no Americans, no perfect fear, no danger, only politics. It would be like an old whore going back for a reunion and finding her sisters crumpled up and tossed aside like old wrapping paper and the young ones sticking their smooth legs out of new doorways.

'Remember the time you let Caryl bring his air rifle to the picnic and he shot that poor crow,' Jessica said to Cynthia. 'Just its wing was broken and it came flopping down the slope. It stopped on that crumbling parapet over there and sat cawing pitifully until Teddy finally took the gun away from Caryl and shot it through the head.'

'It was awful.'

'Caryl was always like that,' said Cynthia. 'When he was ten he told me that he wanted to join the navy and blow up ships.'

'Too many movies.'

'Such a darling! Who was it he married?' asked Angela.

'You know Maude Cameron, who used to live in Bareilly and came up to visit her husband's grave every month. Her daughter was in London, working as a cocktail waitress. Caryl had a two-day stopover in London on one of his flights. They met and started talking. She remembered Debrakot. Her mother used to bring her along when she came up. The next time Caryl was in London, he looked Suzy up and took her out to dinner. They were married two weeks later. It came as a surprise to me, you know, but she's a nice girl and Caryl's going to quit the airline next month so he can spend more time with her.' They all listened so pleasantly, like a row of smiling cats.

I could just hear them, if Cynthia had suddenly left. They would have started talking about Maude Cameron and then her daughter. After a while it would have come out that Suzy had been working as a dancer in a topless bar. There would have been stories about her because someone else had been in London and by chance met her before Caryl had and the news had reached India quickly, where it flourished, like a weed. When the men heard about it they probably chortled among themselves and said that if she was anything like her mother it would be worth going all the way to London just to see her blouse come off.

I wonder what they said about me in Allahabad. Thank God Mother died before she had to suffer with my reputation. We have no privacy because there are so few of us. I remember running into a friend of Daddy's in Calcutta. I was drunk and singing with some rowdy Americans in a bar off Chowringee. He was drinking in the corner and I don't remember who he was. I couldn't recognize him at the time, but I knew he was from Allahabad. His face was very familiar and from the way he looked at me I could tell he was thinking about Daddy and what he would have said. He finished his drink quickly and left. I remember realizing when I saw him go out of the door that the news would soon be in Allahabad and that I could never go back there again. Sitting with the officers' limp arms dangling over my shoulders, being rocked back and forth in time to their songs, I stared at the vacant corner from which the familiar face had been watching me and got a perfect image in my mind of the ladies in Allahabad, relaxing in their wicker chairs, drinking tea, and talking about poor Natalie and how she had gone bad. I have never been back to Allahabad.

Angela took out a set of pictures from her bag and began passing them around. The ladies all nodded and sighed in approval. Cynthia took some snapshots out of her wallet and soon each of them had her own children and grandchildren circulating around the circle. I glanced at each, purred, and passed it on. It was just like a card game. Jessica won with the latest snap of her granddaughter chewing on a pacifier. It got the most squeals. She beamed with delight, the victor. I wasn't even dealt a hand.

'I wish all of the children could come back for one grand picnic,' said Cynthia. 'Wouldn't it be wonderful with everyone here together again?'

'Oh, they'll never come back to Debrakot,' said Angela.

'But they do remember it. Caryl always writes to me and says that some day he is going to bring Suzy up to Debrakot and show her what his childhood was like.'

I met Teddy right after the war, at a New Year's Eve party at my aunt's house, in Calcutta. He had just come back from the Sahara and was full of stories about tanks and Pyramids. We didn't talk much at the party but I knew that he wanted to see me again, from the way he smiled at me through a conversation he was having with someone else. He took me to a movie, projected onto the whitewashed wall of the officers' mess. In those days he was a Lieutenant Colonel. I was impressed.

The Americans were gone and they and the war had left me older and less pretty. Teddy got me right at the tail end of my beauty, like a corsage the morning after a dance, its colours still bright but ready to fade at any moment, its perfume still strong but laced with the smell of cigarettes and brandy. He too was on the edge of youth, with his jowls getting pouchy and his hair greying in front of his ears. He had his whores in Cairo, I'm sure, so I've never felt sorry for him or guilty.

'We've both had our adventures,' he said, 'and like good adventurers we'll never tell each other what really happened.'

At first I had thought I would confess to him about the others, but after he said that, I decided he didn't want to know. One time I asked him what Cairo was like.

He said, 'Probably not much different from Calcutta, except that there we were Englishmen and here we're Indians.'

When he asked me to marry him, I hesitated. I went to a doctor before I said yes, to make sure. The doctor said I should just keep trying.

I think that Teddy wanted a whole platoon of sons to march out from between my legs and follow him into the Sahara, leaving me to wave a white handkerchief and cry. We tried hard to have a child but I knew from the beginning that I couldn't. I didn't tell him for a long time because I was scared he would stop trying.

Two years after Teddy and I were married, he brought me to Debrakot, to the house we have now. He was stationed in Bareilly and would come up to visit every free moment he got. Sometimes he couldn't even stay the night but we tried anyway. He must have waited with his paws in the air for a letter from me saying that I was pregnant. He would come up exhausted from work but always with an eager look in his eye. I could see that he was thinking that maybe this time . . .

I am eight years younger than he. He was in Bareilly for about eight years and then retired early because of a bad liver. After he got out he started the orchard and we tried even harder. I wanted to tell him the truth. I wanted to say, 'Go find some other woman and prove to yourself that it's I who can't have a child. You're as good as any of those men, as good as Kenneth Thatcher and the pilot from Iowa. You're better than them.'

When I finally told him, he already knew; he didn't act surprised. He only looked out the window through which we had both stared so many times at the blurred outline of the hills. Some nights they were distinct and so clear that you could almost see the trees, and other nights, when the moon was thin or not at all, it would take a long time to make out their velvet shapes.

'I'm sorry,' I said.

'Don't say sorry to me. We're both in this together.'

'No, Teddy, we're not. It's not your fault. I've known for a long time. You could have a child by someone else but not by me.'

He kept looking out the window. His arm was under me.

'I'm like a mule,' I said. 'Cross-bred and sterile.'

'Shut up, Nat,' he whispered. 'It doesn't matter now anyway.'

I remember one Christmas in Allahabad. I wanted a doll like the one the English girl in the bungalow two down from ours had. It was almost as big as I was, with red cheeks and blonde curls. It was porcelain and the girl's mother had sewed frilly dresses and bonnets for when the English girl took it riding in their tonga. I remember watching them ride by me on the street and seeing the doll sitting between the little girl, whose name was Sheila, and her mother, who was the wife of an army officer. I used to sneak over to their wall and pull myself up so that I could see into their garden. Sheila and I never played together. I don't think she even knew I lived close by. She never waved. I would stand there peering through the tangle of shrubbery which framed the lawn and the house. Sometimes Sheila would be playing in the yard and the doll was always with her. It was her only playmate. My mother told me not to go there unless I was invited but I went anyway, to see the doll. One day Sheila left it leaning against a grapefruit tree at the edge of the lawn. It was alone. I climbed the wall and crept over to touch it. The mali saw me and called out. I ran and hid in the bushes. He was a nice man but he wouldn't let me touch the doll. He lifted me back over the wall and told me never to come back.

For Christmas Daddy brought me a doll from Calcutta. It wasn't like the English girl's. It had a wooden head, with painted black hair. It was fat. The clothes it wore were pale and ugly. It wasn't soft or warm, like I imagined the other doll was. I was angry with it and refused to hold it. Mother sat it in my chair at the dinner table. I threw it onto the floor. Mother spanked me and sent me to my room. She left me alone in my room and put the doll next to me on my bed. I threw it off after she went out. I lay there crying, listening to them eating dinner and laughing. My uncle and his wife were there and so was our neighbour old Mr Griffin with the purple nose. I lay sobbing on my bed for a long time, looking at the doll sprawled face down on the brick floor. Suddenly my anger flowed into me again and I jumped up, grabbed the doll, and ran outside to the garden. There was a tank of water near the gul mohur tree which was used for irrigating the flower beds. It was a green-umber colour and full of frogs. I threw my doll in. It floated. I bent down and pushed it under, as if I were trying to drown it, just like we did with our Alsatian's puppies when she got crossed with the pi-dog instead of the stud which came all the way across town, in a tonga, to mate with her.

Mother came into my room and slapped me. I was lying on my bed staring at the wall, as if there were something between me and it. They had fished my doll out and it now sat bedraggled, the paint peeling off its face, its clothes stained and limp; a pool of water had dripped on to the floor. Mother left me alone again, this time with the door locked. I lay perfectly still, exactly as before, my face still stinging, but no tears.

Slowly my head turned to look at the doll. It looked worse than before. It was ugly and its clothes were as torn as Ummi's, the sweeper's daughter. I lifted myself on to my elbows and swung my feet off the bed. Slowly I moved towards the doll. Its face looked like the face of the leper who used to beg outside the church on Sundays. My hands touched it. It was wet. I grabbed it and then hugged it tight against me. It felt cold and hard against my chest. I stood in the middle of the room holding it. Mother came in after a little while and found me still standing there. I remember she began to cry and hugged me like I was hugging the doll.

When Lionel was born, Millie came up to stay with us. He was her first child. It was summer and the heat in Lucknow scared her. We stayed up late nights talking about it, after Teddy fell asleep in his chair with a novel over his face. She came up to Debrakot looking like a buffalo, her belly swelled out in front of her. I made her lie on the sofa, with pillows under her back to take the weight off. She would lie like that and tell me that secretly she hoped it would be a girl, even though out loud she wanted a boy. Millie was still a schoolgirl back then. She wanted to dress Lionel in skirts when he was young, just once, to see what her daughter would have looked like. I told her not to because I said it would make a pansy out of him. I sat there in the chair beside her, wishing my belly had ballooned out like hers. I tried to count in my mind how many children I should have had by then, how many had been stolen from me. They would all have been boys.

'Nat, I wonder what it will be like,' she said.

'What part of it?'

'The whole thing. It seems so strange and makes me feel like an animal. What am I going to do after it's over? Do I lick it clean? Will I hold it under me and snarl at the doctors.'

'Of course not,' I said. 'You'll trust the doctors.'

'I won't. I didn't even trust Charles the first few nights we slept together.'

'Don't worry, Millie. It'll all be quite civilized.'

'No, it won't,' she said.

'Come on, we're people, not dogs.'

'Will I have to eat the placenta?' she asked with a smile.

'Shut up, would you,' I said. 'Teddy will wake up and hear you.'

'He'd get upset because he doesn't know anything about it.'

'You're being silly.'

Millie looked up at me from the sofa. 'You wouldn't understand either, Nat. You've never had a child.'

'No, I haven't,' I said. Teddy woke up with a start just then, the novel falling off his face. He grunted and looked at the two of us, with a tired expression. I stood up and took his hands. That night I tried very hard to get a child. I kept thinking about Millie and when I finally fell asleep I dreamt that I had a child too, which I carried around in a sack like a spider.

When Lionel was born, I was there in the room with Millie. I watched the whole process. Millie came out of the hospital after a few days. Whenever I held him she would snarl at me as a joke. I think she got jealous, though, because I spent so much time with him. After a while her playful snarl turned into an earnest frown and at any excuse she would take him away from me.

Lionel was my son also. He has come back to me. He formed in my uterus and then was stolen from me just as they steal a pearl out of an oyster. Men stole him from me. I slept with them and as I dreamed about him they reached in and pulled him out just like poachers stealing quails' eggs. Men are all poachers. Lionel was mine but they took him from me when I fell asleep. Again and again he formed inside of me like saliva. But they always robbed me of him.

It was always Lionel, the same little boy with the Christopher Robin sandals on his feet and his hair fine as silk, blowing carelessly in the wind. He has come back now as a man. Still I think of him as a young boy whom I will dress every morning in a clean pair of half-pants and a patterned shirt. I will wet his hair and comb it so that it is moulded to his scalp. I will buckle his sandals and then watch him run down the steps of the house into the yard, his face as ruddy as a plaster cherub's. He will call me Mummy and ask for barley sugar.

Lionel is both my child and my lover. I want to hold him and him to hold me.

His face is delicate, his eyelids like the thin petals of an orchid, the purple veins showing through a membrane, his eyelashes like stamens. His eyes are round and have seen nothing. He is my baby. His eyes open and search me, dark and liquid, flowing into me. I stare back at him, fixed in his vision. His eyes ask me to follow him to a ruined cottage, and make love to him under the chestnut trees. His little hands, eager to grab at my fingers, are as wrinkled as an old man's paws which have felt for everything and now, cut and gnarled with experience, are his eyes. His fingers are innocent, with tiny pink nails. They clutch a chestnut, explore its shiny surface. They fondle my breasts and caress inside my thighs. His fingers comb my hair and tickle me. They probe. They become fists and pummel me. He is cute. His lips close over my nipples and suck milk out of me. I hold his head in my hand and watch a contented smile crease his cheeks. His lips are harsh and his tongue rough like a cat's. He moves like a leech down my neck to my shoulders and then to my breasts. He is handsome. I brush his black hair flat and kiss his forehead. He is narrow and strong. He chirps happily, drools and mutters in my arms. I pat his tummy. His skin is dark. He smells of soap. I listen to him whimper and moan.

He leads me into a mango grove, moving ahead of me like a shadow, beckoning from behind each tree, and I run after him, getting younger with each stride, feeling my hair grow long and thick, my legs stronger and faster, and my breathing less and less strained until we reach the centre of the grove and Lionel turns to me, no longer a shadow, a man who folds his arms around me, stands a moment, completely still, laughing and handsome in the moonlit grove, full of mysterious trees, with a stream running through it and a pavilion in the centre, with flagstone floors and a marble dome, peacocks filling the branches of the mango trees and calling to each other sympathetically like mourners at a burial, a row of banana trees along the back wall, waving their wide leaves like punkahs, the sky full of constellations, so that when I look up at Lionel I can see above his head the seven sisters, hovering over him like a crown; I break out of his arms and run to the edge of the stream, splash water at him and then grab a sapling by its slender trunk and bend it over me like an umbrella until he stands up and chases me and we both run through the grove like playful deer, falling finally exhausted in the moss at the foot of a huge mango tree, out of which come peacocks to dance in front of us, and Lionel plucks a feather out of one and sticks it in my hair as we lie in each other's embrace and watch the pavilion fill with musicians who begin to play lutes and sing, conjuring out of the stream a cobra which sways in time to their music, its head pivoting slowly and its tongue flicking like fire; Lionel leaps up and runs to the bank, grabs the serpent by the nape of the neck and begins to wrestle with it in a dance, dragging it out of the water, with its long body coiled about him, its white fangs slashing at him like swords and he dodging as it strikes, dancing out of reach like a mongoose until, catching it off guard, he grinds his heel into the cobra's spine and then steps nimbly back to watch it twist frantically, dancing itself to death. The musicians speed up their music and now they are playing in a frenzy, the notes coming off their instruments like sparks.

*

Lionel was still sitting under the chestnut tree. His face was turned away from me and I could only see half of him. The shadows had grown out of the trees like new branches. They crept up the slope towards us. I sat and watched them approach like vipers. I waited until they reached my feet and began to swallow me. I stood up, my drunkenness collecting inside me like mercury in a thermometer. After a few steps I began to run.

He turned just before I reached him, his face shocked. I dropped down beside him, reached a hand up and touched his face. He was like a statue, frozen into a heroic pose. I wanted to see him fight again.

'I want to see you fight the snake,' I said.

His bewildered eyes shone, with the brightness that coal must have just before it turns into diamonds. I grabbed him and began saying things to him.

'You're my son, not Millie's, Lionel.'

'Hold steady a second,' he said. 'You're drunk.'

He began to stand up. His hands held both of mine but he was going to leave me. I would be left again, as I've been left so many times.

'No!' I shouted. 'Don't leave me, Lionel. I'm too old now.'

'What are you talking about?' he asked.

He began to step away from me. He let go of my hands. I jumped on him and began hitting him. 'Damn you,' I said, 'damn you, Lionel.' He caught my clenched fists in his hands, holding them like two pieces of fruit in front of him. His fingers wrapped like tentacles around me. I couldn't escape his grip. He held me away from him. 'Lionel!' I screamed, but he was not looking at me. He was looking over his shoulder up the slope where the picnic was going on. Teddy and Angela were coming down towards us. I fell on my knees. I began to cry. I remember feeling their hands coming at me but I don't remember their touch. I had passed out by then.

There was a little rain while I was asleep, probably the first of the monsoon showers. It has cleared the air so that from the veranda, where I am sitting, the plains are visible until a long way off. The mountains are beautiful. In the morning they are always blue. When there is a haze they are the colour of smoke; they even look like smoke. This morning there is no haze and their blue is not that of smoke but of fire, the colour at the centre of a flame. Latif brings me a cup of coffee and says that Teddy went riding at five. That means he will be back in another hour. It also means that he is angry. Whenever he goes out riding at five, I know he is angry. I sip my coffee slowly, ignoring its taste, engulfed by the mountains which are my home and my exile.

Lionel is probably still asleep. The orchard stretches down the slope below me; the apricots, plums, and peaches are ripe. The boys are out early picking.

What happened yesterday? It was another boring picnic. I made a scene; but then, I was drunk and that excuses it. They will talk about it but that's all right; they always do. The only person I feel sorry for is Lionel. He didn't know what was going on. I embarrassed him.

I can hear Angela and Stephanie talking between themselves.

– She really must not like Lionel. It's too bad.

– No, it was just because she was drunk.

– But it came out. She hates him.

– Well, I guess it embarrasses her, but mostly it was the gin in her.

– Maybe it was. You do silly things when you're drunk.

– Like play badminton.

They will both laugh and wonder how I'm doing this morning. It wasn't just because I was drunk. I don't hate Lionel, either. Was I thinking of Charles? Lionel does not look like his father but he reminds me of him.

We were on a hunting trip together in Assam. Charles and Millie had been married about a year. In fact, we celebrated their anniversary on the trip. Teddy shot two massive boars and Charles bagged a nice sambur. One night just after the sun had gone down and the forest began to sound like a cocktail party, Charles decided to go out and shoot a peacock. We could hear them just a little way off in the forest. They were in the branches now, settling down for the night. I asked if I could join him and he said, 'Why not? Just don't make any noise.' Teddy was tired. He had no reason to worry. Charles had gone to school with him and was still in love with his own wife. Millie was going to come too, but after she saw how dark it was, she stayed behind. There was a little path from our tents which snaked through the shrubbery for a way until the forest opened up into a glade with a pool of stagnant water in the centre. There was a ring of thorn trees around the glade and it was in these that the peacocks had roosted. I held the torch and Charles shot two. They landed on the ground with a dull thud and fluttered a little.

FOUR . *Farleigh*

In most towns the graveyard lies on the outskirts. Whether out of a fear of ghosts or their own death, people tend to bury their corpses at a distance. But in Debrakot the graveyard was planted in the centre of town, with the streets and houses all around it. In fact it seemed to antedate the town, as if it had been there before anything else and the buildings had grown up because of it.

Farleigh's grave was empty. We were grouped around it. Our black clothes seemed a pathetic gesture of respect to a man whom none of us knew. I don't think anyone really cared whether Farleigh was dead or not. He meant as much to the people there as the pile of red dirt which had been dug out of the hole to make room for his coffin. We stood quietly, though, and listened to Padre Joseph stumble through the service in his thick south Indian accent. Four of the men lowered the coffin into the grave. The ladies threw the flowers they had been clutching onto the coffin and began to walk away. At a signal, two of Padre Joseph's sons began to shovel the dirt back into the hole. Mrs Augden had taken my arm. The Brigadier walked ahead of us. The town appeared to be completely deserted. Behind the curtained windows I could imagine faces peering out at us curiously. Silently we dispersed.

Gaining entrance into the last few days of a man's life is like breaking a flower from its stem. No matter how great the man or how beautiful the flower, the end is inevitable and quick. Its termination is unpleasant. Coming to Debrakot, I was entering the ends of people's lives, without having known their beginnings. It was sometimes like walking through an unplanted graveyard, the holes dug and waiting. I was young; I was twenty. I had entered their sequestered lives like a bee gathering pollen out of withered blossoms. I sat and waited for them to fall off their stems. We spoke the same language, with the same accent. We had the same colour skin. We had the same traditions. The only difference was that I felt as if their end was mine, that my traditions would die with them and I would be left alone, an orphan. During moments like that, I would say to myself, 'Hang tradition, hang it all. I've no need for it.' But when that empty feeling passed, I would turn around and say, 'Maybe I will carry part of it on.' I am like a refugee escaping from his home. On the road out I find my people dying before me and take what is valuable from them, adding it to my load. When I die, someone will take the valuables out of my pack and walk on. We are all refugees escaping from our tradition and yet, at the same time, carrying it on our backs.

The rain had begun in June and was still falling in August. It seemed as if it never stopped.

The mountains were crisscrossed with paths, most of them forgotten and unused. I took one of these trails one morning and followed it uphill until it crossed over the hump of the ridge and began to descend on the north side. The undergrowth became thicker. At places the path was completely washed out. When I was just about to turn around, I noticed a little distance ahead the trees ended and there was some sort of a glade. As I drew closer, the outline of a building appeared through the maze of trees. It was an old bungalow, built much like the others in Debrakot. It was in bad repair. A section of the wall had collapsed and part of the roof was caving in. It had been patched up with a haphazard arrangement of corrugated tin and beaten-out canisters. All except one of the windows were intact.

At the edge of the forest, I crossed a small stream which flowed into the glade and collected in a pool near the bungalow.

I didn't think anyone lived in the building. The grass around it was up to my knees. The door stood ajar. I walked in to explore. A strong, sour smell of mildew hit me as I entered. There was a long corridor, menacingly dark and silent. The plaster on the walls crumbled away when I touched it. At the end of the corridor there was a square window, admitting a pale grey shaft of light. A torn runner led me down the hall. I could see three doors on the right, sunken into the wall.

The first of these doors opened easily. The room I entered was much brighter than the hall. Stepping inside, I looked down at my legs. There was a bloodstain on my trousers. As I began to roll up the cuff, I suddenly let out a startled cry. Attached to my leg was a cluster of leeches. Their slick black bodies were fat with my blood. One or two had gorged themselves and seemed to be stretching contentedly, waving their tapered heads in the air. I tried to pull one off and it slipped out of my hands. It felt soft and watery. I grabbed it again but by that time it had affixed its suction cup to my skin and no matter how hard I pulled it remained glued to me. Its elastic body stretched like rubber and squirmed in my hand. As if at a signal all of the other leeches suddenly raised their heads and began waving. While I was trying to pull them off one grabbed on to my finger and, before I could stop it, lodged itself between my fingers. I shook my hand frantically but it clung to me.

I remembered that salt was the only way to make them let go. Though nothing hurt, I limped out into the hall and tried the next door. It led me into a sparsely furnished living room. I looked around for salt but there was nothing in sight that would do. At the far end of the room there was an open door. I staggered over to it, imagining I was losing blood by the gallon. There was a kerosene stove and two or three pots and pans on the table. I found a salt shaker.

The first leech I tried it on curled up into a tight ball and then, spurting blood, tumbled off my leg. With relief I sprinkled some of the salt on the one between my fingers. He died the same way. One by one I killed them. The final casualties were twenty-six dead. I was wounded. At each place they had affixed themselves a slow trickle of blood oozed out. By the time the massacre was over, my socks and shoes were soaked in blood. I watched the last leech die an agonizing death. I had begun to enjoy it. They lay strewn about on the cement floor. Suddenly I realized it was my own blood, not theirs. At the thought, the back of my throat went sour.

When I turned around to leave, I was surprised to find a bed piled high with filthy blankets and quilts. From under this mountain protruded the gaunt little face of an old man, scruffy with a week's whiskers. A shock of yellowish white hair spread on the pillow like a mane behind the tiny head. I could hear a slight breathing, high and wheezy. Occasionally his lips quivered. Except for that, he could have been dead. I slowly crept over to him. One of his arms lay outside of the covers. I could almost see the bones through his transparent skin. On the inside of the elbow the skin was raised in a cluster of welts, some of them scabs, some fresh and raw. It seemed as if a needle had been stuck into his veins a number of times. He slept soundly, as if under some narcotic. Was he an addict? There didn't seem to be room enough for the needle to fit in any more. I wondered if I should wake him and find out if he was all right. Was he sick? I stepped back and out of the room, deciding to leave him alone. The leeches were forgotten.

I remembered them again when I reached the front door and stared across the grassy meadow which had looked so innocent when I approached the house. I felt light-headed and wondered if it was from loss of blood or the shock of finding the old man. My legs were still bleeding. I knew that the meadow was infested with leeches and that I was sure to be covered with them by the time I got back home. Finally, with a quick gulp, I raced through the grass as if I was being chased and didn't stop until I reached the trees.

Mrs Augden had me bathe my legs in warm water. She dabbed each of the bites with antiseptic and bandaged them. They itched.

'I met a strange man,' I said. 'Well, really I didn't meet him. Actually I found him. He was asleep.'

'Where?' asked Mrs Augden.

'In a broken-down bungalow on the north side.'

'That's Farleigh. I wouldn't go there again.'

'Why not?' I asked.

'He's queer.'

'He seemed sick,' I said.

'Only in the head. He's as tough as a goat. I can't see how he survives out there by himself, eating nothing that's good for him and little besides.'

Two or three mornings later I was again standing at the end of the overgrown trail, debating whether to explore it once more. Ever since I had seen the old man I had wanted to meet him. The forest was a bright green. Even the mist seemed green.

The bamboo swayed in a feathery dance. Emerald doves perched in the dense foliage and shiny green pit vipers slid like trickling water through the heavy grass. The oaks seemed more sinister this morning, their arthritic shapes bent over the path like a dark tunnel. I stood there on the edge of my imagination, arguing with myself. It was a cold morning and the mists were circling above me in the forest.

I saw a movement up the path. For a moment I thought it was just the mist but then the outline of a person appeared. As he came down towards me through the long tresses of grass, I began to make out details. It was the old man. I knew that even before I saw his face. It was a face pale enough to be part of the mist. His hair made him look particularly ghostly, it was long and straight, scattered about his shoulders. He wore a frayed straw hat with the brim pulled down over his eyes. From a distance he seemed to have no features at all, but when he came closer, I could see the narrow line of his lips, creased over his gums. His eyes were transparent blue. The skin on his face was taut and I could trace the outline of his skull through it. He wore a long black overcoat which reached to his ankles and buttoned from the knees up. It obscured everything but his face. Occasionally his hands would emerge from the sleeves like hermit crabs creeping out of their shells. He wore canvas shoes without socks and carried an empty cloth bag slung over his shoulder. He waited until he was a few feet away from me and then nodded.

'Who are you?' he asked unpleasantly.

'My name is Lionel,' I said.

The old man gave me a queer look. His pale blue eyes made me feel completely exposed. He coughed and spat without once taking his eyes off me.

'I'm Farleigh.' His voice was thin and wheezy. I waited for his hand to come out of its black sleeve but there was no sign of it. We stood there for a moment looking at each other. My eyes drifted down to his feet. Three leeches were attached to his ankle. A trickle of blood had stained his canvas shoes.

'You've got leeches on your foot,' I said.

'I know,' said Farleigh. 'They're feeding.'

'Shall I put some salt on them for you?' I had begun carrying a bag of salt in my pocket.

'No, no,' he said. 'They'll do no harm and drop off when they're satisfied.'

'I got twenty-six last week,' I said. 'They itch terribly.'

'Twenty-seven,' said Farleigh. 'I counted them.'

From the way he looked at me I could tell he knew I had come to his house. He made a sad little sound which came from the bottom of his throat.

'Do you play caroms?' he asked.

'I haven't in a long time.'

'If you'd like to play a game or two with me sometime, you're welcome,' he said softly.

'I'd like that,' I said, not meaning it.

'Why don't you come tomorrow afternoon around three o'clock.'

'All right, I will.'

'I must go to market now,' Farleigh said, and stepped past me. He headed towards town along the main road. The skirts of his black coat flapped against his ankles. I couldn't help thinking of the fruit bats that flew into the electrical wires at night and burned to death. I used to see them every day in Lucknow, clinging to the wires like wilted flowers, their black wings wrapped around them, waving in the wind. They used to dangle above me, morbid decorations. My friends and I used to take our cattys and try to knock them down. We could never break them loose, for they clung to their death like the last few leaves on a dying tree cling to the branch and refuse to let go. I can still hear the dry, solemn sound of our rocks pelting their black shapes and the shrill cries of our frustration.

Farleigh led me through the dark hall into his living room. This time I had a chance to look around the house carefully. It was in worse condition than I had thought. The walls were cracked and the roof was mapped with stains where the rain leaked through. Where the beams joined the wall there was a vine growing out of the plaster. Along many of the cracks and especially on the window sill, moss grew in patches.

'Will you have tea?' asked Farleigh.

'If it's no trouble.'

He vanished into his bedroom.

I explored the room carefully, leafing through some of the magazines and books that were strewn around on the floor. There were pictures on the wall but the glass covering them was powdered with dust, so that I could see only ghostly images of the paintings and photographs. One above the fireplace made me curious. I brushed the dust off the glass with my fingertips. The face leapt out at me. It was Farleigh as a young man. His features were sharp and clearly defined. He had a ruddy complexion and his hair was a dark colour. The old man seemed to have faded. It was as if all of the blood had been sucked out of him. What made me recognize the photograph was the stern, almost fanatic look in the eyes. They were not as pale in the photograph, a slate grey, but as intense and penetrating.

'How long have you been in Debrakot?' asked Farleigh as he entered the room with two cups of tea.

'Two months,' I said.

'And where did you come from?'

'Lucknow,' I said. 'I'm living with Brigadier Augden and his wife, they're friends of my parents. Probably I'll take over his orchard for him.'

'How do you like Teddy Augden?' asked Farleigh, and then, without giving me an opportunity to answer, he continued, 'He's a bastard.'

'I can see how someone could think that,' I said.

'He's the sort of man who loves his dogs more than his wife. He came up here and started yelling at me one day for no good reason. I told him he could get the bloody hell off my land. He's an officious son of a bitch. These fellows that get into the military think because they've got stars on their shoulders they've a right to order others around. I showed him.'

'You've lived in Debrakot a long time,' I said.

'About ten years, but always out here, away from everything. I never had a wife, so I didn't get in on any of the gossip. It's a quiet place and the loneliness slows the time down. Each year gets a little shorter than the one before it. They race through you faster and faster until you can feel them pulsating against your temples. They become a whirlpool and suck you in.'

Farleigh stopped a moment and thought. All the time he had been talking, he had been scratching his elbow through his coat.

Carefully he pulled up the sleeve until his forearm and elbow were visible. There were half a dozen leeches feeding on him. That was what had left the marks I had thought were caused by needles. Gently Farleigh brushed the leeches off on to the floor. The bites hardly bled and I wondered whether anything remained in the blue veins which formed patterns under his transparent skin.

'I'm sorry, Lionel, I've been talking like an old man,' said Farleigh, without mentioning the leeches. 'Let's play caroms.'

I watched as he dragged a heavy carom board out from behind a chest of drawers. He placed it on a low table between us, blew the dust off, and then disappeared through the door again. He returned with a cloth bag full of caroms and a small can of talcum powder. He doused the board with the powder. It was the same sort of powder my mother used to use, a strong lavender smell which almost obscured the mildew smells of the room.

I ran the palm of my hand over the smooth surface, spreading the white dust over the entire board. The caroms were spilled on to the table and the two of us arranged them in the centre, black against white and the red one in the middle. They looked like a surrounded army. Farleigh let me take the first shot. I smashed the strike directly into the cluster of caroms and watched them scatter. A few flew off to the sides but none ducked into the corner holes. Farleigh studied his shot as if through a fogged window. Finally his gnarled fingers snapped and sent the strike ricochetting off the side. It connected with a black carom and sent it skittering over the powdered surface. He swore under his breath. His lips were open and I could see his tongue licking his gums. Farleigh seemed to have been sucked dry, humped over his side of the game like the brittle husk of a cicada.

In my mind I saw our game going on forever, the two of us sitting across from each other, alternately flicking the caroms back and forth. Time would dissolve. As days passed and then weeks, the only sound would be the caroms ricochetting off the sides of the board. We would be pinned to our chairs. Death drains a person of his strength, his soul, his spirit. It is not a poison or an infection. One of our servants died of a gangrenous stomach. His belly and intestines swelled out so that it looked like he had swallowed death. I was about twelve when he died and I remember seeing him lying on a cot in front of his quarters with a sheet over his bloated body, moaning like a cat does when it's in heat. I remember his face a few weeks before he swelled out. His eyes receded far into their sockets and the bones of his face jutted out behind his stark features. It seemed as if he was being drained. Nobody knew that he was dying but I sensed that there was some evil hovering around him, sucking the life out of him. Then he began to fill with pus. I wondered what it was, a bat, a snake, a wildcat? Finally a doctor came. He arrived in a tonga at the gate of the compound and all of us children followed him to the dying man's house. He went inside and shut the door. Two hours later he came out, with his coat hanging over his arm and sweat glistening on his bald head. He looked straight ahead and at no one. The servant was dead. When we saw his body it had shrunk. The sweeper was called and made to take a basin of pus and blood out to the garbage dump and pour it into a hole. We children were told to stay away.

The corpse looked so small. We had thought of him as fat but with the pus drained out of him he was nothing. What had done it? Maybe the doctor, I thought, he was like a parasite. Maybe the doctor was like a vampire who came at night and drew blood from the dying man. The story was that as soon as the doctor cut the man open and began to let the pus out, the servant had died. Some said the doctor put his mouth to the hole and sucked the infection out and spat it into the basin. I didn't know what to believe. My parents told me that doctors didn't kill. Maybe he wasn't a doctor, something else in disguise. After it was all over and the stories were heard at least three times by everyone and settled into the anthology of memory, I began to realize in a simple way that death was outside of a person, a foreign animal. It attached itself to you and was a parasite, killing while feeding itself.

I stared at Farleigh as he calculated his shot, where the strike would hit the wall and at what angle it would return to knock the caroms into the pockets. His face and hands had the same shrivelled appearance. I realized then that he was about to die. It was startling. The veins on his temples seemed ready to burst with his concentration. His skin looked like tissue paper. I wondered what was left in the veins. They were blue as if filled with ink.

We played for three hours. After a while the games began to spill into each other. Farleigh would begin setting up for a new game as soon as the last carom had gone into a pocket. He had stopped talking after an hour and soon after that his eyes stopped searching me. They were blank. Their sky colour changed to the colour of clouds and misted over. His breathing became louder and his hands shook when he lifted them off the table. He looked weak. It was as if every shot drained him of a little bit of energy and gradually he was losing consciousness.

I shot quickly and then waited patiently for him to fire. Each time he waited even longer than the time before. His body slumped lower and lower.

Outside it was getting dark and there was hardly enough light for us to play by. I imagined the shadows to be creeping in on us. Neither of us could move from our chairs while the caroms formed and re-formed – an army on parade. They seemed to move without us, black and white discs spinning on the powdered surface, moving back and forth on their own accord. Both of us sat transfixed like statues while the game played itself. We were immobilized. Then I saw the leeches coming into the room. They were a dark, waving mass. I couldn't tell them from the shadows, except that they moved faster, like a wave spilling over a beach. Once in a while their oily black bodies shone for a second. They came into the room like a migration, over the window sills, through the cracks in the wall. Some of them wriggled up out of the floor. All of them were sleek and hungry, a bloodthirsty mass, hugging the ground. I thought I felt the first ones reach my feet...

Farleigh fainted, not as I have seen some women do, with a moan or a sigh, but gently, like a baby falling to sleep. His head dropped to the carom board and his hands sank down beside him like wilting leaves. I studied him for a few minutes but the room had become so dark that his features were indistinguishable. His skin seemed almost luminescent.

I carried him into his room and laid him on his bed. He weighed hardly anything and I could feel his bones through the heavy black material. I undid the buttons of the greatcoat and was surprised when I found he was completely naked underneath. He looked like a shelled walnut. It was a strange sight, his hairless, pale body, the size of a thin child. It almost glowed in the dark. The coat was spread beneath him like a bat's wings. Quickly I covered him again and pulled the pile of dishevelled blankets over his sleeping form.

I ran across the meadow again, lifting my legs high. It began to rain as I reached the hump of the ridge and I was soaked through to the skin when I reached the house.

The Brigadier was sitting in his usual chair, smoking a fat cigar and drinking rum. I came downstairs after changing into dry clothes and asked the cook to bring me a cup of tea.

'Take some rum instead,' said the Brigadier. 'You'll catch a cold. Where the hell were you? I just about sent a search party out.'

'I was at Farleigh's place.'

The Brigadier grunted. 'My wife said you'd been there.'

'Who is he?' I asked.

The Brigadier inhaled a cloud of smoke. It filtered out of his nose and mouth as he talked.

'He's a bastard,' said the Brigadier. 'I wouldn't see him again if I were you. There's something quite wrong with him upstairs. He's a . . . oh, what do you call them? . . . a sadist. Yes, that's the word, a sadist. Thank God he has his house on the north side and keeps to himself most of the time. Be careful if you go there.'

'Has he done anything?' I asked.

'Oh, plenty of things. Only one time was I involved. Three years ago I had a beautiful spaniel, a cocker, as gold as a sovereign. That was his name, Sovereign. A strong little dog who could flush a pheasant right into the barrel of your gun.

'We were out hunting on the north side close to Farleigh's house, when the dog suddenly disappeared. It was just at the end of September. I shouted and whistled but Sovereign refused to come. He'd never done it before. I rode up and down the trail but there was no sign of him. Finally I decided to search around Farleigh's bungalow. As soon as I came into the clearing, I could hear the dog whining. Farleigh had him tied to a peg near the pond. Sovereign was friendly and never bit anyone. The old son of a bitch had muzzled him, though. He was wearing that black coat of his and was squatting by the pond, catching leeches in the mud. He had about fifteen in a bottle and was just about to put them on Sovereign when I rode up. But I had come too late. The dog was already covered.

'Farleigh dropped the bottle and ran inside. I tried to catch him but he locked the door behind him and wouldn't come out.

Sovereign was bleeding. I untied him and then began pulling the leeches off one by one. It didn't hurt him and he kept licking his blood and wagging his tail. But he was weak and I carried him home even though he wanted to run.

'As I was afraid would happen, he got leeches up his nose, and though we stopped the rest of the bleeding and fed him meat and vitamins, the leeches in his nose refused to come out. Every day I tried but they would slip out of my fingers or the tweezers. He began to cough up blood and got sick. It was frustrating because the devils would poke their noses out of his nostrils and wave around but as soon as you grabbed at them they were gone, far up inside his sinuses. Sovereign kept losing blood. After about a month he finally died.

'I caught Farleigh in town one day while he was buying vegetables. He began to squeal when I hit him and threw turnips and tomatoes at me. But what more could I do than scare him? He just squealed like a trapped bird, stammering out some excuse about the leeches being his pets just like the cocker was mine and that he had to feed them somehow.'

'He's crazy,' said Mrs Augden, who had just walked in. 'The servants say that he takes children from the nearby villages and covers them with leeches.'

'Rubbish,' said the Brigadier. 'Dogs but not children. They'd kill him if he tried it.'

All that night I thought about Farleigh and wondered over the Brigadier's story. Farleigh was lonely. I knew because of the way he had invited me to play caroms. I wondered whether the loneliness had driven him mad or if he had been that way to start with. Nobody knew anything more about him than that ten years ago he took over the bungalow from an alcoholic Scotsman. He had never tried to get along with anyone in Debrakot. His pension kept him alive and he could draw credit from the provision store in town.

There seemed to be nothing dangerous about him. Unless he had some supernatural powers, I wasn't threatened. He could never muzzle me and tie me to a peg. Why had he tortured the Brigadier's spaniel? I found it hard to believe. Could it really be that he was feeding the leeches? Were they his pets? How could anyone feel anything but disgust at a leech? Then I remembered the way

Farleigh had let them feed on his arm. They were pets. But they were killing him.

I wasn't frightened of Farleigh. I was frightened of Debrakot. Farleigh had lived by himself so long that he could just as well have been dead or alive. It didn't matter to anyone, least of all himself. It was a ghostlike existence, passing through the world like a phantom, unseen and unheard. He looked like a phantom with his pale skin. You could almost see through him. Maybe that was what the leeches were for. They sucked the blood out of him, so that he could be transparent. It was as if he was made of glass, so that once the blood was gone, he became invisible. That's all a hermit wants – to be unseen.

That night I stood by the window. The pale vapours flowing over the mountains reminded me of ghosts. The sky was so clear that the stars glinted. It was as if the clouds had settled on to the mountains, like a collapsed tent. A steady wind tossed them from ridge to ridge. When the mist parted it exposed dark gaps of shadow and occasionally a ridge was left bare, a strip of light and black. The mist was all white, naked and sensuous. It seemed alive and suddenly swept up the mountains towards me. It stopped in the pines below the house and rallied for a moment. Then with what seemed like a sudden impulse, the moonlit clouds rushed down again and dispersed into patches, glowing islands among the black waves of ridges.

I felt deserted on one of those islands, like a shadow in a bright light, nothing more than just an absence of light. Some day I would be like Farleigh, a figure in the mist, nothing more than a shadow or a silhouette. In the day Debrakot was green. At night it was white, a bleached landscape. I felt like an intruder, a dark shadow in the green sunlight and a black form in the misty night.

On one of the closer islands of mist I saw myself, cast like a shadow on a white screen. I was wearing Farleigh's black coat and his straw hat with the brim pulled down over my face like a beak. I was the last person in Debrakot, alone with myself. My body was moving in a regular rhythm. I was digging, shovelling earth out of a hole and piling it to one side. It was a grave and for a moment I thought it was my own. Then I put the spade down and lifted a corpse in my arms, dropped it into the hole, and then covered it up.

This was the last death in Debrakot. It left me completely alone, the youngest, now the oldest as well. When the burial was finished I walked away through the mist, gradually becoming less and less distinct, almost transparent, and then invisible.

'I bought this house from a melancholy Scotsman. The night before he left we sat in this room drinking and he told me the story of the place and how he had got it.

'It was built by a Major Braithwaite. He was a young officer and liked to come to Debrakot for his hunting. Those were the days when the town was full of parties and gaiety. I remember the point of those parties was to get a pretty widow drunk enough so that she was willing but not so drunk that she began to cry.

'The Major fell in love with a young woman who left Debrakot three days later on her way to Calcutta, to sail for England. They were mad about each other but her parents took her away. The Major moped around for the rest of the season and then returned to his post in the Punjab. He had a sketch of the girl which he took everywhere with him. It's now hanging over there by the door. I don't know who drew it or whether it's a good likeness or not. Have a look at her. Wipe the dust off.

'Major Braithwaite caught a fever after a few weeks on the plains and was sent back to Debrakot on a medical certificate. He was very ill and they did not think he would make it home alive. When he reached here he was put under the care of the civil surgeon, an ancient doctor whom the whole town was afraid of.

'The doctor examined him on arrival and prescribed two or three medicines and regular bleeding by leeches every morning and evening. His bed was right here where the sofa is, according to the Scotsman. He lay here for five days. His servant was the only man with him. The Major had the picture put up where it still hangs, so that he could watch her as he died.

'The servant collected leeches from the pond outside and every morning he would place them, as the doctor had instructed, all over the Major's body. It was to drain the poisons out of his blood. Some were put on his temples, others under his arms and in his groin. They were left there until they gorged themselves and dropped off. It's not that silly an idea. Leeches suck out the bad blood, the unhealthy toxins. Some people say it's folk medicine and superstition but it works. They have the same effect as a tonic. The new blood rushes into you and makes you healthy.

'But leeches weren't enough to save the Major, probably nothing could have kept him alive. He died five days after coming back to Debrakot, staring at the sketch, with leeches fixed at spots all over his body.'

I had gone over to the framed drawing and rubbed away the dust. The girl was pretty, with her hair in a bun, exposing her long smooth neck. She had a smile on her lips and her eyes were wide and watery.

Farleigh had stopped talking and was rolling up the sleeves of his coat.

'See,' he said. 'I let them suck my blood for a little while every day. It keeps me healthy.'

'It's killing you,' I said, taking a deep breath.

Farleigh frowned and shook his head, flicking one of the leeches with his finger so that it reared up angrily.

'That's what killed the Major,' I said. 'He lost too much blood when he needed every drop he had.'

'You think it's superstition just because it's an old idea.'

'No, it's ignorance. You don't know what you're doing.'

'Try it once,' said Farleigh, taunting.

'I won't,' I said, feeling nervous.

'Why not? They won't hurt at all.'

'You're dying,' I said. 'Do you know that? And the leeches are killing you.'

'No, they're keeping me alive. For ten years they've kept me alive. I came to Debrakot to die, ten years ago. A doctor in Bareilly said that I had not more than a couple of months to live. When the Scotsman told me that story, I thought I'd try the leeches. They worked. The doctor said that no medicine would keep me alive. But the leeches did. Give them a try.'

He stood up and came towards me, holding his arm out for me to see the leeches.

'I don't need them,' I said foolishly. 'I'm not dying.'

'Of course you are,' said Farleigh. 'Why else did you come to Debrakot?'

He pulled one of the leeches off his arm and held it out to me. It wriggled in his fingers.

'Come on. It really works.'

'You don't understand,' I said. 'I don't need any medicine.'

'Of course not. The leeches are much better than any medicine.'

I was backed against the wall. The old man stared at me with his head cocked to one side. The leech dangled in front of me. Slowly he raised it to my face.

'I'll cure you,' he said, 'Trust me, I'll cure you.'

'No, no,' I said. 'That's not necessary.'

His hand moved in front of me as if he were choosing a place to put the leech. Then he reached out. As I felt the squirming leech against my neck, I yelped and raced out of the room. Nothing stopped me. I was across the meadow in a few seconds. The leech was glued to my neck and I had to pull at it to get it off.

Yesterday I tried to stop myself from visiting Farleigh. Curiosity and maybe thoughts from the night before, a desire to answer my own fate, led me up the overgrown path.

This time I went out of fear. A heavy rain cannonaded upon the forest. I slogged through the ankle-deep streams which flooded the path. My umbrella did no good, the drops coming in from all sides. My clothes stuck to me. My hair was pasted against my forehead, and dripped a steady stream down the bridge of my nose.

I was scared of what I had said to Farleigh. Perhaps I would find him sitting quiet, alone and happy in his living room with the leeches sucking contentedly at his elbow. Maybe not. I felt guilty and ashamed about running away from him, even though he had gone mad and tried to put leeches on me. It was not a fear which repulsed me but a sense of danger that drew me closer to him. It was not daring, though. The feeling pulled me up the path. It was the same sort of feeling that tugs at you when you are standing at the edge of a cliff. It is not suicidal either. I wanted to see Farleigh again and find out if he was all right but I also wanted to face him and not run away this time. If he held out a leech again I would let him put it on me. Farleigh was harmless. I was afraid of him, though. He and I had both come to Debrakot alone. In him there was something of myself which I wanted to find. He was a hermit.

But Farleigh was dead. He lay beside the pond with his sallow face upturned against the beating rain. It seemed to have washed all of the colour out of him. He looked almost like an albino except for the blue tint in his eyes.

I stopped beside him and noticed that there were leeches grouped around his throat almost like a necklace. With uncertainty I unbuttoned his coat. The material was swollen with the rain and it was difficult to undo the buttons. When I finally got it open, I wished I hadn't. The leeches covered him like smallpox. There were hundreds of them dotting his body, drinking up the last drops of blood in his veins. His body was translucent and the rain seemed to soak right through the skin. I wondered to myself whether he had fallen at that spot or lay down there on his own. He had watched them come inching out of the pond, waving their noses in the air. Had he felt them crawl over his body and take hold?

Mrs Augden clutched my arm as we walked through the deserted streets of Debrakot. She was silent. The funeral seemed to have depressed her, not because of Farleigh but because it was simply a death like any other, like the one which would kill her and the rest of us.

I wanted to shake her off my arm and run away down the hill. But she held me as if she would never let go. I was suddenly afraid. Her grip was painful and I felt as if she were feeding off of me.

FIVE . *Hotel London*

1.

Three days in Debrakot seemed like a year. My room hadn't been occupied since the hotel closed in 1958. I lay on my bed and stared at the spider webs lacing up the corners of the ceiling. My stomach muttered and I reached down to massage the dome of flesh which rose and fell with my breathing. It didn't feel a part of me; it was as if I was a weak and skinny fellow pinned down by an enormous weight. I looked down at my arms and they seemed swollen. My fingers were bloated and my wrists bulged. Was it all part of me? My thumb traced around my navel and then moved down the curve of my belly. My hands felt as if they were moulding a mound of clay. Why didn't it tickle? If someone else had touched me there I would have jumped. I belched and tasted spices at the back of my throat. My insides roared with indigestion. What an awful dinner, watery chicken curry made with too much chili and rice that had stuck together in globs and tasted like glue. The cook claimed he used to work at the hotel when it was running.

I lay thinking, almost in conversation with my stomach, which answered me in gurgles, growls, and once in a while a disagreeing burp. The Hotel London was a sprawling wooden structure, looking like an ornate beehive. It had six tin spires, all but two of which were broken. Twenty years of neglect had left it dirty and almost ruined. The floors and furniture, all good sal wood, were still sturdy but, outside, the grilles and railings were rusting away, the garden had been overrun by a galaxy of white hydrangeas, and the tall iron gate was wedged half open and refused to budge in either direction. The thought of renovating the place seemed absurd.

Where was I to start? A sharp pain seemed to puncture the wall of my stomach. I unbuttoned my trousers to relieve some of the pressure. The idea of a walk appealed to me. It might help my digestion. But then I remembered the hills. Damn it, why wasn't there somewhere level in the town, where I could walk without wheezing?

Content to remain a prisoner of my body, I went back to massaging the dome, caressing it gently every time it growled. My grandmother used to explain the noises to me when I was small. She said there was an animal inside of her which grew larger the more she ate. Her stomach swelled out from below her bosom like an enormous bolster pillow. She used to hug me tightly against her belly and spongy breasts until I thought for sure I would suffocate. 'Do you hear the animal inside of me?' she would ask. 'Doesn't it snarl like a tiger? Some day the animal inside of you will grow this big.' Then she would laugh and stroke her thighs happily.

My grandfather was a queer man, one of that sort who didn't know where he belonged. He was a pious Muslim, never drank, prayed regularly, and fasted during the holy days. He knew Persian and loved to recite Hafez and Sa'adi. But he wore European suits and knotted a tie every morning. He smoked Trichinopoly cigars and had a white beard. His hair was clipped short and greased down with scented pomade.

My parents lived in Delhi but I hardly ever stayed with them when I was young. I went to boarding school in Dehra Dun and as soon as classes finished for the summer I was packed off to my grandparents' in Debrakot. Here I was my grandmother's prisoner. The memories are vague and leave a bad aftertaste. The house stood behind the hotel on a knoll overlooking the town. It was a collection of dismal rooms, smelling of fusty blankets, damp plaster, and cigars. The odour of a 'Trichi' cigar still sends me into a panic. I look around to see if a white beard is advancing on me. But my grandmother would never have let him beat me. She would squeeze me against her huge tummy and murmur archaic couplets in my ear. She would make me promise her that I was never going to leave and go home to my mother, but always stay with her. Now, thinking back, I realize that she was mad. One year when I was in high school she killed herself. It was all very innocent and she didn't make a fuss beforehand. They found her dead in her room.

There was a little bottle lying on the floor which the servant girl admitted having brought from the pharmacy. But she swore she hadn't known what it was. My grandmother had just sent her along with a note. The pharmacist claimed the note said that the poison was needed to kill a dog. That was the end of it.

I would sit in my grandmother's room all day and she would send the servants for snacks and sweets. In those days there were kababwallas on every corner, barbecuing skewers of meat over charcoal braziers. If we went out for a walk we would stop two or three times along the way and my grandmother would order me a plate of kebabs and then, always as a second thought, one for herself. That is my only happy memory of Debrakot and I was sad to come back and find the kababwallas gone.

We didn't go outside much and I was never allowed to roam the town by myself for fear that I would fall down and fracture a bone. My grandmother was kept in purdah. Out of doors her massive shape was draped in a black gown with a hood and a veil of lace to see the world through. I think she hated to be hidden like that and preferred the seclusion of her room to the concealment of her bourka. Alone, the two of us would sit on her bed and she would sew clothes for me and dress me in expensive outfits, red satin blouses bordered with Kashmiri lace and stitched in gold thread, round hats made out of rabbit's fur, and tight-fitting trousers which clutched my legs painfully.

I heard footsteps coming down the wooden floor of the hall. I thought it was the cook or maybe the caretaker, who had only one eye, and didn't believe me when I told him that there was a road being built to Debrakot. A knock rattled the door.

'Come in!'

When I looked up, I was surprised to find a man my age standing in the doorway, looking at me with a peculiar smile on his face. I quickly buttoned my trousers and tucked in my shirt.

'Hello,' I said. 'Are you a ghost?'

'No,' he said, 'not that I'm aware of.'

'In that case, find a seat and sit down. I'd love some company. This town is dead.'

'Most of it.'

'My name's Salim Ahmed. Yours?'

'Lionel. I hope I'm not intruding. I saw your light on and I was curious. This place has been deserted ever since I've been here. You're not a tourist, are you?'

'No, I own this hotel, or at least my father does,' I said.

Lionel nodded. His face was long, the skin pulled down tightly over the contours of his skull. The bones were prominent behind his smile and his eyes had a cloudy look about them. But they were friendly and welcomed my stare. His hair was reddish brown and fell from a centre part down both sides of his forehead. He was an Anglo-Indian. His face seemed to be one of those amorphous faces, so plain it was startling.

'What do you do here?' I asked.

'I manage an orchard,' he said. 'Apples mainly.'

'You sell them on the plains?'

'There's no one here in Debrakot to buy them.'

'Have you lived here always?'

'No, originally I'm from Lucknow. It's been two years since I settled here.'

'It seems we're the only two people in this town.'

Lionel laughed. 'Yes, if you don't count half a dozen old farts, nostalgic types, pensioners, and dotty widows. Are you staying long?'

'My father has sent me to start the hotel up again. It's sort of his last attempt at moulding me into his image. I'm no businessman. For some reason he persists in trying to give me jobs. You'd think he'd give up. I guess he figures I can't do too much harm to this pile of ruins. In Debrakot I'm out of his sight, which he'd be happy about. He also thinks there might be some profit in the hotel, now that the road is coming. It will bring tourists to Debrakot.'

'Ah, the road. Everyone's waiting for it,' said Lionel.

'You aren't?' I asked.

'No.'

'Come on, it will spark some life in this town.'

'There was a time when I imagined that I'd live here by myself forever. I manage the orchard for a retired Brigadier, a friend of my father's.'

'Doesn't it bore you to be alone so much of the time?' What he had said made no sense to me. I had no idea what he was like. He had come out of the darkness and still seemed like a piece of the darkness, the black silhouette of a personality.

'I like the quiet and the seclusion,' he said.

'You're lying,' I said, trying to get him to show himself.

'Maybe that's true, but you don't know me yet and I don't think you've been here long enough to appreciate Debrakot.'

'Long enough to know that there's nothing happening here. Look, I've met people like you who say they want to be alone all the time. Poets, dreamy types, who smoke their cigarettes down to the filter. It's nonsense. You'll always find them sitting at tables in restaurants waiting for someone to come along and interrupt their solitude.'

'Debrakot is beautiful, though, with its silence, its mountains, only the birds . . .'

'It's an eclipsed world, Lionel. The road will change that . . . for the better,' I said.

'The road will ruin this town. It will bring in the plains people. Just think of the history that will be destroyed.'

'What history?' I said. 'There's nothing left.'

'This hotel. I walked into it and I felt as if it was a hundred years ago.'

'It's dead. All of it is rotting away. You're deluding yourself, Lionel,' I said.

'I'm a scavenger.' He lowered his voice. 'The sort of person that lives on dead things.'

'Don't get morbid,' I said, feeling my spine tighten like a spring.

Lionel stood up and moved to the window. He moved like a phantom. I could almost see through him.

'Will you have some tea?' I asked.

'Of course,' he said.

We walked downstairs to the kitchen, where the cook had already spread out his bedroll and was preparing to go to sleep. He complained when I ordered a pot of tea and some biscuits to be brought to the billiard room.

'Do you play?' I asked, pointing at the arsenal of sticks and balls in the glass cupboard.

He shook his head. For a few minutes we knocked the balls around, both shooting at the same time, getting a feel for the game. The room was dimly lit, with two or three lamps on the walls. Over the pair of tables there were bright bulbs with wide metal shades. They shone on the green felt surfaces and made the rest of the room feel even darker than it was, stretching our shadows out of proportion.

'Shall we play snooker or billiards?' asked Lionel.

'Is there a difference?'

'Oh, a tremendous difference. In snooker you try to keep the balls out of the pockets and in billiards you try to put them in,' he said.

'Whose rules are these?' I asked.

'My own, of course. I told you I'd never played.'

'Why don't you try to keep them out and I'll try to put them in,' I said.

'That's called snookerds, or billkers, whichever you prefer.'

'Snookerds it is,' I said, and began to fire away as fast as I could at the pockets. Lionel took his cue and began shooting the balls away from the holes. For fifteen minutes it was complete war. I had it the easiest and put most of the balls in during the first few minutes. When it was reduced to two or three balls, the game grew wilder. We began chasing round the table, trying to get the right angles for our shots. Both of us started shouting back and forth. Finally there was only one ball left. Our cue sticks tangled together and the ball danced in between them. At one point I had almost pushed it in when Lionel knocked my stick away and picked the ball up in his hand.

We began fencing with the long sticks, just missing the lights and jabbing at each other.

'Touché!' I yelled, and tried to jump on to the table. Miscalculating, I landed half on and half off the table, with one foot in the corner pocket. My knee hit a leg and felt as if it was broken. Lionel stabbed me gently, twice in the stomach, and scampered away. There was a fireplace at one end of the room with a broad mantelpiece. From a chair he leapt on to this perch and stood with his chest puffed, taunting me to attack. I rolled myself off the billiard table and ventured into the fray again, shouting like a musketeer. We duelled for a few minutes until I collapsed on the ground and conceded at cue-point that Lionel had beaten me.

'But I'll get my revenge next time, don't worry,' I said, 'and even cheating won't save you.'

At that moment the cook walked in with the tea, trying not to look surprised.

Lionel poured the tea and then helped me to a chair.

'God! I should lose some weight!' I said.

'I don't know, it kind of makes you interesting.'

'Thanks, I suppose that's a compliment,' I said. I was actually flattered. 'Do you know something, this is the first meeting of the Debrakot Chamber of Commerce,' I said.

'What?'

'You and I are the founding fathers of this city. Your orchard and my hotel are the basis for this city. When the road comes, we're going to be here to greet everyone.'

'I'll chase them away!'

'Shall we start a Rotary Club?'

'Oh God! You're not one of that sort.'

'We'll make this town into the greatest hill station that ever was.'

'Why don't we sabotage the road, Salim?'

'You and I can run Debrakot. We'll be kings!'

The next morning at about eight, Lionel met me in front of the hotel. We walked back to his house through the deserted streets. The morning was brilliant, the air laced with a slight breeze, and the sun warm and soothing. Between the houses along the street I caught glimpses of the plains below, faintly visible under the haze of dust which lay like a dirty veil over the entire panorama. Lionel was in good spirits and kept complimenting the day as if it were a woman with a new hairstyle.

We had breakfast on his porch. Sitting in the shade of a trellis overwhelmed by wisteria, we watched a hoopoe lancing the ground with its beak, searching for grubs. It was the first good meal I'd had in Debrakot and I ate twice my share. There was toast and omelettes, paranthas and curried potatoes, and fruit from Lionel's trees.

'You can't tell me Delhi has mornings like this one,' he said.

'No, you're right, but don't you get lonely by afternoon?'

'Morning is the best time, when nothing matters and I can just sit here and dream. I go to sleep by nine and I'm up at five. That way I avoid most of the lonely hours.'

'But last night . . .'

'That was unusual. The evening felt especially long and I wasn't tired enough to go to bed. I decided to take a walk and that was when I saw your light.'

'You were lonely, admit it,' I said, swallowing most of my third cup of tea in one gulp.

'I was, but not in the way you think. If I hadn't met you I would have walked on a way and then turned around and come home. I was happy to be alone.'

'Go to hell,' I said. 'You wouldn't have come up to my room if you'd wanted to be alone.'

'I was curious,' said Lionel.

Friendship is a process of admitting things. Gradually we revealed ourselves. That morning we talked about the differences between our two worlds, Debrakot and Delhi. I invited Lionel to visit me in Delhi. He hesitated but then promised he would. For a week we were together. He showed me his orchard and helped me explore the hotel. I was even coerced into riding with him one morning. It was fun even though the insides of my thighs were raw for two days afterwards. The things we did together would have bored me in Delhi, long walks in the hills, games of caroms and ludo after dinner, and endless conversations over cups of tea. In the end Lionel told me why he was there. It didn't come out like a confession but more as a matter of fact. He was telling me how he hated cities and that Delhi would probably be just like Lucknow.

'I'm sure it isn't,' I said, 'but what's wrong with that?'

'Since I was young I lived in a city. My mother had a small garden and that was where I grew up, sheltered from everything outside our walls. From the beginning I was afraid of the city, even though I lived in the heart of it. I was never a part of Lucknow, separated from the streets and bazaars. But the city always loomed on the other side of the wall, vicious and threatening. Debrakot, on the other hand, is like a huge garden where I can roam alone without fear. The hills enclose and protect me.'

'What is there to be scared of in a city? There is crime of course, and the danger of getting run over on the street...'

'That's not it,' said Lionel. 'It's the world of alleys and narrow lanes I'm scared of, anything outside the garden wall. Have you ever wandered into the gullies, Salim? Where the women are kept, hidden away from the rest of the world. There are rooms in which widows are kept and unfaithful wives, their dead or angry husbands' prisoners. In those dark rooms, under mildewed blankets, the women sit like dead stalks of corn. The air in those rooms is fetid and evil. They can only hear the mice scuffling in the corner. I fell in love with a girl in Lucknow.'

'Oh yes?'

'And the city snatched her away from me. One moment she was in my arms and the next minute the gullies had sucked her into their maze. I hunted for her down every street, through the entrails of the city, but she had disappeared forever. After that I knew that I could never live in the city again. I came here, to live in quiet.'

Lionel told me this one afternoon while we were inspecting his trees. I felt strangely jealous or angry towards the girl. I wasn't sure why. She had driven Lionel out of my world into the hills. But in a strange way she had brought us together. That night we had met, he had been thinking about her and had wandered into my room. We both needed each other. With him, Debrakot seemed suddenly bearable, a shared exile. I began to think seriously of running the hotel, whether it made money or not. The town and Lionel's friendship would give me a fresh start. I felt possibilities begin to rise inside of me. I felt ambitious and excited. I felt thin. The walking in the hills would be healthy. I would lose weight through exercise.

The caretaker's milky, blind eye winked in spasms when I told him to cut the hasp off the door where my grandfather's belongings were stored. He still didn't believe that I had come to start the hotel again. My father had hired him fifteen years ago to guard the place and he kept it locked up like a dungeon. He was like a man confessing secrets. Over and over, he explained to me that the doors had been kept fast since the day he was hired. I assured him that I trusted his word and it really didn't matter.

'A car!' I said, as the doors of the godown swung open.

In the centre of the shed stood a dark blue De Soto. All four of its tyres were flat and the canvas roof was rotting away with mould. Dust powdered its elongated body but the chrome still glinted proudly. Lionel arrived just as I was admiring it.

'What? Has the road been built already?' he asked.

The caretaker explained that my grandfather had bought it from an English Colonel who had a house on the Mall. He had brought the car up to Debrakot on the backs of fifteen coolies. That was a long time ago, before partition. The Colonel used to drive it back and forth along the one wide street which ran from the Hotel London to the municipal library. When he left to go back to England, my grandfather bought it to drive guests through the gate of the hotel.

The rest of the godown was packed with boxes and trunks. Lionel seemed eager to open everything there at once. I held him back and suggested that we take each trunk at a time and replace everything before moving on. Most of the trunks contained clothes and furnishings from my grandparents' house. Lionel found a pair of my grandmother's pantaloons. He made me hold one side of the waist and then stretched them out. They reached from one wall of the shed to the other.

'My God, I think they'd fit you,' he said.

'Get lost.'

'Hey! Look at this.' Lionel said. His head was thrust into a deep wooden chest. After a few seconds he pulled out a box of cigars.

'My grandfather smoked those continuously,' I said. 'He thought he was Churchill. That's probably what killed him.'

'Shall we try one?'

'No, they're awful.'

'Come on; be brave. One cigar won't hurt you.' Lionel took a box of matches from his pocket and stuck a cigar in his mouth. He had a satisfied grin on his face. He was enjoying himself. I had to take a cigar. Lionel's glowed like a phosphorescent worm. He lit mine. I felt nauseous and scared, holding the 'Trichi' in my hand as if it were a bomb.

'What's wrong?' asked Lionel. 'It tastes good, a little sweet.'

'They're dipped in rum. My grandfather never drank but that was his one concession. He did it himself and I remember they used to be lined up to dry on the porch every Sunday afternoon.'

'Go on, try it.'

'I can't,' I said. 'It will make me sick.'

Lionel encouraged me and blew a cloud of smoke in my face. I started to lift the cigar to my mouth but just as it was about to touch my lips I gagged. It felt like more than just a revulsion towards the cigar. My whole body seemed ready to leap out of my mouth. It was as if someone had reached down my throat, taken hold of my stomach, and was going to pull me out of my skin. I put a hand over my face and threw the cigar far away into the back of the shed.

Another spasm bent me over and I puked on the floor of the godown. Lionel grabbed me and helped me outside. The air felt clean and I shut my eyes and tried to forget the cigar, Debrakot, and Lionel. Sitting down on a parapet, I stared across at the plains, wishing the hills would flatten out in front of me.

The fire started as an insignificant spiral of smoke. The caretaker, who had been squatting alone against the wall of the shed, noticed it first. He gave a little yelp and rushed inside. My cigar had landed behind the trunks and had lit some old papers or rags. I yelled to the caretaker to bring a bucket of water. He and Lionel disappeared around the corner while I tried to move the trunks aside and get at the flames. The trunks were heavy and my head was still spinning from the cigar. My arms felt weak and disjointed against the weight of the trunks. I heard a frightening, crisp sound and the smoke began to spume out with a sudden rush. Collecting all my energy, I dragged the final trunk from between me and the fire. Then I realized I had nothing to fight the flames with. A wave of water drenched me from behind. Another splashed beside me. Lurching out of the black smoke, I ran into Lionel and the caretaker holding empty buckets in their hands. I wanted to laugh.

My lungs felt as if they had been pumped full of soot. The inside of the shed was now black with smoke. It was hopeless. The sides of the shed grew red hot and the windows popped one by one, as if someone had shot them out with a gun. A crowd gathered, people I had never seen before, more than I had thought lived in Debrakot. As the flames spread to the main building, we moved down the hill to safer ground and watched the whole hotel catch fire, storey by storey. I was still coughing. Someone gave me water. I couldn't see them because my eyes were streaming with tears. I wasn't sure whether I was crying or whether it was because of the smoke. My emotions were on a trapeze. The first thing I saw when my vision cleared was a squadron of bats scattering from a window in one of the spires. They shot into the sunlight like blowing cinders. Two or three regiments of rats evacuated through the drains and we watched them scurrying away down the hill. Several children chased them with stones and clubs, screaming and laughing.

From the beginning I had felt laughter at the back of my throat. I held it back for a while but then it burst out like hiccoughs. Two or three heads turned in my direction. I began to cough. It seemed so typical, so predetermined. I thought of my father scowling at me and telling me that I should have been more careful. He would say again, as he had said so many times, that I should try to be more responsible.

Gradually a feeling of pain and grief suffocated my laughter. My grandfather's pride, the Hotel London, destroyed in a few hours. I wondered if Lionel was feeling sorry about all of those 'wonderful old things' he had liked so much. Fire is ruthless with history. I thought of the caretaker, who had kept everything locked away for fifteen years. He was watching the greatest secret of his life explode. I looked around. There was the cook with his bedroll under his arm. He had rescued it just in time. I remembered my own clothes. Nobody could retrieve them now. Beside the cook stood the caretaker. His blind eye winked at me accusingly. The other eye wandered over the mass of smoke and flame. A breeze came up from the plains at that moment and whisked the blaze into a swirling gyre. There was a hoarse, rasping sound and the entire hotel seemed to turn into a hurricane or tornado.

Lionel came up to me. His face was black with smoke. In his hand he held my suitcase.

'How do you feel?' he asked.

'Guilty,' I said. 'Did you go up to my room and get that?'

'Yes, I figured you'd want these things. I know my clothes wouldn't fit you.'

There was a muted explosion and one of the spires flowered into orange flames. A few seconds later another spire lit up, followed by each of the six in turn. It looked like an enormous candelabra or birthday cake. Soon the ground floor began to collapse and the Hotel London seemed to settle into the fire, in an almost grateful gesture. This was the end of Debrakot for me. There would be nothing to come back to. I was between regret and relief. My whole body ached. There was nothing to do but watch it erode in the red, orange, and yellow climax. The hotel had commanded the mountain, all of Debrakot, for over forty years, and in one brilliant flash, it was gone. I felt a current of fear pass through me, as if I had just killed something. I imagined my grandmother. She was standing beside me and I was hanging from her hand like a pet gibbon. She was dressed in her black bourka and only if I looked carefully could

I see her dull, grey eyes behind the lace, dancing over the flames. Her death had been something like the burning of the hotel, a helpless accident, uncharted, innocent, and irresponsible. It had been a furious act carried out with grace and dignity. There was something dignified about the hotel as it roared with fire. I looked beside me and my grandmother was gone. I saw her black shape moving through the smoke, climbing over the burning timbers. She moved slowly, with a slight waddle. I could see her for a few minutes as I stood transfixed. Then like a phantom she was gone, carried away with a flurry of smoke on a breeze.

2.

The traffic was congested as we approached Delhi. Trucks were lined up along the side of the road. Jhandah Singh, my driver, kept his hand on the horn the whole way, edging in and out of his lane. The sun was setting over Delhi and it glared right in our eyes. It seemed to lacerate the sky. I bent my head and held my fingertips over my eyelids. Lionel sat in the front seat, hunched against the door. He was snoring quietly. I was impatient, eager to get home but frightened to see my father. What would he say about the hotel? I had decided to tell him myself as soon as I got home. It might have been easier sending him a telegram but there hadn't been time. The sweat dried on the back of my neck and my pores stung with salt every time I moved. I tried to shade my eyes with a newspaper but the glare seemed to burn through everything. It was incessant and irritating. My trousers had hitched up and my thighs felt constricted and sore. Where my waistband cut into the folds of my stomach, the skin was raw. Undoing the buttons of my shirt, I lay my head back on the seat and tried to go to sleep. It was impossible. I was too nervous. My fears grated against my mind.

About a kilometer on we turned off the crowded highway and jostled over a rutted culvert onto an unpaved road. The dust billowed up in clouds around the car. The sun was still in our eyes, a little to the right of us now. I bent over and put my head on my knees. The dust seeped up through the floor and after a little while I could taste it on my lips. My entire body began to itch. The muscles in my back were quivering and for a moment I wanted to scream. There was a dry tension in the air. I could feel the dust under my fingernails. I needed a bath, a cold drink, and sleep. I didn't want to see my father or anyone. I didn't want Lionel to wake up. Why had I invited him? All I wanted was to be alone. I heard myself whimper. The inside of my mouth tasted sour.

'Thank God!' moaned Jhandah Singh as the sun suddenly dropped behind the minarets of the Jummah Masjid. The whole scene, the flooded fields covered with a layer of water chestnuts, the buffaloes wallowing in the irrigation ditches, the lines of egrets moving across the pink sky in formation – everything seemed subdued. The dust gave the landscape a pastel quality. I sighed and ran a hand through my hair. The Jumna came in sight. We crossed over the new bridge and joined the rush of cars and bicycles. Now that the sun was out of my eyes, I felt so much better. I could breathe again and the irritations subsided.

Just then I remembered Karim. He was the servant boy at our house. Only fifteen years old, he was an expert masseur. Under his fingers my entire body was like putty, flexible and yielding. The thought of a massage cheered me up even more and I lay back into my seat with a sigh of expectation. My muscles began to shiver as they relaxed.

I only saw my parents for an hour. They were on their way to Calcutta and had to catch a train that night. We talked in their bedroom as they packed. My father said hardly anything at all. He showed his anger and didn't say goodbye when he left. My mother scolded me in a piercing voice, each word a needle. As soon as they left I shouted to Karim. He came trotting up the stairs and salaamed politely.

'Come,' I said. 'Kill me.'

Karim's fist kneaded the soft flesh at the base of my spine. The touch of his fingertips crept up my back, rib by rib. He had complete control over me. I relaxed. He tightened me up and then relaxed me again. Sometimes his hands were gentle like rain. Then it would feel as if he was cutting me open and pulling the meat away from the bones. I would moan and he would giggle. The sockets of my shoulders and all my joints felt as if they had been dislocated, pulled apart and strewn on the bed. Finally I groaned and Karim went to get me a glass of buttermilk. As I was drinking it, Lionel walked in.

'What's happened to you?' he asked.

I moaned and sent Karim for another glass of buttermilk.

'Have your parents left? I had a wonderful bath.'

'They've gone. Why don't you have a massage? Nothing like it,' I said.

'No, thank you. I'd rather not. He might sprain something. Was your father angry?'

'Yes. He didn't say much.'

'Did you tell him the truth?'

'No, but he suspects it,' I said. 'I told him it was one of the kerosene lamps that fell over.'

'Well, there's nothing much he or you can do about it,' said Lionel. 'What about dinner?'

'We'll eat out. The cook hasn't got anything for us.'

I hauled myself out of bed and pulled on a fresh set of clothes. Jhandah Singh drove us to the Khyber restaurant, near Kashmiri Gate. We took a table on the top floor in the back. The food took time coming, so we nibbled at the dish of pickled ginger and drank Coca-Cola.

'Well, how's Delhi so far?' I asked.

'It's different from Lucknow, bigger, busier, but not as frightening. The streets are wider. It's more modern.'

'I thought you didn't like modern things.'

'I haven't said I liked Delhi,' he said.

'But it's exciting, isn't it, all of the people around you, so many faces.'

'They're impersonal, though.'

'Impersonal people are better than none at all.'

'I don't know,' he said. 'The only people I want to come to Debrakot are people I know intimately. It's like a secret place when you were a child, a grotto, a hidden cave where you put your favourite objects. Only your best friends knew about it.'

'We have places like that here, restaurants, theatres, swimming pools we like especially. There are places where my friends and I go all the time, as a ritual.'

'Is this one of those places?' asked Lionel.

'Yes, in a way.'

The food came after a long wait.

'Ah, what food!' said Lionel. 'You're bribing me, Salim, but remember, my heart isn't in my stomach.'

'Mine is,' I said, slicing off a chunk of lamb from the Full Leg Barra. 'As long as there is good food, I don't care where I am. Taste is my most developed sense. It's almost an emotion for me. Some people have good eyesight. Others can smell as well as animals. I knew one chap who said his fingers were more sensitive than other people's. A musician has a developed ear for notes. For me a meal is the most enjoyable experience in the world. It's like a good novel. There's a beginning full of expectation. You and I sitting here waiting for the waiter to come. I put the Keema Nan in my mouth and I remember the familiar tastes; the lamb has new flavours for me, hidden spices and subtle textures. Everything climaxes when all of the tastes combine in my mouth. Then there will be the satiated hour or two following dinner with the lingering aftertastes and a full, contented feeling of happiness. That's what I live for.'

As I was talking a group of people came up the stairs. In the half-light of the restaurant, they looked vaguely familiar but I couldn't be sure who they were. As they came towards our table I recognized them. They were old college friends of mine, Munoj, Teddy, and Sylvia.

'Hello,' I said.

'Hey, look, it's Salim.'

'Hi, Fatty, eating again?'

'Keep shut!' I said, laughing and shaking hands. Their insults stopped hurting me long ago.

'Where have you been?' asked Munoj. He was a thin, lively fellow, whom I liked a lot. Munoj played cricket for St Stephens when we were all there together. Teddy and Sylvia were cousins. She was beautiful in a peculiar way. Her face was like one of those three-dimensional pictures which change expression when you tilt them. Laughter flashed on and off her face and the only part of her which remained still were her soft-boiled eyes, wide and wet. Her long black hair fell below her shoulders and coiled around her tight breasts. She was slim and tiny, nervous all over except for her eyes. They seemed to soak into you.

There was the usual gossip. I didn't introduce Lionel till a few minutes into the conversation but Sylvia had already slipped into the seat beside his. She likes to flirt and I winked at Teddy and Munoj. No one had succeeded with her so far, though we had tried. She was not the sort to attach herself to one person. I think it pleased her to hold more than one man on a string. She had us threaded around her like a necklace. After a while we had given up and just played her game, drank deeply of her eyes, and rebounded smiles and compliments without taking it too seriously.

I told the story about the hotel and we shared our food with them while they waited for theirs to arrive.

'God, your father must have been mad,' said Sylvia.

'No, of course not,' said Munoj. 'It's nothing to Fatty's daddy if a hotel burns down. There are plenty more.'

'Go to hell,' I said.

'It must have been a sight!' said Sylvia, drowning Lionel in her eyes.

'I'm surprised you didn't see it from Delhi,' he said.

'Come to think of it,' said Munoj, 'I thought the sun was setting in the wrong place last Friday.'

'Funny joke!' said Teddy sarcastically.

I was unhappy to see our meal disappear so quickly. I decided to pay them back when theirs came. Sylvia had Lionel willingly cornered in his seat. The rest of us caught up on news, who was in trouble, who was on drugs, and who had stopped smoking. Munoj told us about Dicky Singh's hernia, which he got in a match against Khalsa College. It was a funny story but I couldn't help listening to Sylvia. She was telling Lionel that he must see Delhi properly and that I would show him nothing but restaurants. Lionel was listening to her politely, looking a little surprised and bewildered.

'I'm already stuffed,' said Sylvia, putting a full stop to their conversation. She turned to me. 'We've got to take Lionel to see the Cellar. He says he's never been to a disco before.'

Lionel looked embarrassed and shrugged his shoulders at us. 'Come on, Salim, you're taking us,' said Sylvia, standing up.

'But I haven't finished eating,' I said. I looked at the plates sadly. They were empty – no sign of the waiter. 'I'm tired, we've been driving all day.'

'Nonsense,' she said. 'Come on, pay the bill and we'll shove off.'

Munoj and Teddy winked at me as I left.

Jhandah Singh let us off a few blocks from the Cellar. I told him to go home. Sylvia walked between Lionel and me, swinging her purse like a pendulum and talking in her high, sticky voice. There were not many people out, a few hippies, a couple holding hands but acting as if they didn't know each other. A yellow-and-black taxi burst around the corner, almost knocking down a fashionable young man rattling a key chain in his pocket and wearing a blue cap. The three of us laughed. The man scowled and checked the cuffs of his bell bottoms for mud. Finally the street felt comfortable again and I relaxed. The thought of food clenched in my stomach. I wished I could have had another plateful at least. The night and the city almost made me forget it, though. The Regal Cinema had a detective film showing and billboards claimed it was in its hundredth week. A giant-size hero in an orange turban pointed his pistol at me. The heroine's boobs were eight feet across. We plunged into the discothèque. The band wasn't playing but a record player was turning out scratchy tunes. We found a table in the corner and tucked ourselves into the darkness. Sylvia ordered a drink. Lionel and I had fresh lime sodas.

Being a third person is like being alone. It has always been that way for me, with my parents, with my friends, with anyone. I am a huge nuisance to everyone, I said silently, as I listened to Sylvia telling Lionel about the swimming pools in Delhi. Whenever I get into these situations, I think of getting up and leaving. But then I realize that I have nowhere to go. I am too big to hide under the table. People think that they have an obligation to keep me around. If I was thin they could ignore me.

'How big is your orchard?' Sylvia asked.

'About three hundred acres,' said Lionel. 'It's all on the slope of a mountain.'

'It must be lovely.'

Yes, it is, I thought. Everything for you is lovely, Sylvia, and pretty and cute, because you yourself are lovely. If you had a crooked nose, or no breasts, or worse than that, if you were as fat as I am, there wouldn't be such a thing as beauty for you. There would only be your ugliness, your flaws. I see everything through my fatness. The world is full of beautiful things and they're all thin and graceful, trees which bend in the wind, mountains which taper to peaks, minarets, horses, and most of all, people. For you, Sylvia, Debrakot would be perfect. Your graceful figure would make it even lovelier. I can't live there because I'm gross. I need to hide myself in the city, which is full of those ugly things Lionel talks about. My body hangs on to me like a filthy thought or an obscene beggar. It's a disease. I can't have a private life. I don't fit in small, secluded places. Clothes cover people's bodies but they can't hide mine. Nowhere am I alone except within myself and there I am totally empty.

I'll never be anything. I can't hope to fall in love and have someone love me in return. I can't hope to succeed at what my father gives me because everything bores me. I just want to eat. The frightening thing is that that's all I have to do. It won't be hard. Since I was in school I realized that there was nothing to worry about. My father has plenty of money which is as much mine as it is his. I will spend money and collect a few friends because I spend money. The city will always swarm around me with its faces full of insults, leers, smiles, and laughter. I cannot hide anywhere but at least in a city there is nowhere to be a castaway. That's what I'm afraid of, being a Robinson Crusoe.

'I know the Augdens,' she said. 'I mean, my parents knew them.'

I have a way of escaping at these times. I can dissolve into a fog and ignore everyone around me. It's a state of not thinking. If I drank it would be the same thing. I need people around, though. I can't escape from myself when I'm alone. I melt myself down into a dull, unthinking substance. That's what I become, a metal like lead, soft and lethargic. I'm pliable. People could bend me and stretch me, hammer me flat, and I still wouldn't notice. The music jars me loose from the world, so do your voices, and I float away like a giant blimp. The thick music is hoarse and painful as a cough. I sit buried alive in my chair, drumming on the table with my pudgy fingers, humming tunes, grinning whenever anyone speaks to me but completely dissociated from it all.

'I don't know what the hills are like . . . I've been to Simla a few times on holiday but that was during the summer and the tourists just transport Delhi to the hills at that time of the year. It's not much different. But the loneliness must be relaxing. I'd like to see Debrakot.'

When I am lonely sometimes I want to be completely alone and other times I want crowds around me, filled with voices and sounds. But it doesn't make any difference where I am because no one can come inside of me and know me. The only time I felt full and secure was that week with Lionel in Debrakot. The fire destroyed everything because now there is nothing to go back to and even if there was, I would be a third person. Sylvia, are you really going to take him, rescue him? It was so good when both of us were deserted there together.

'You might get bored in Debrakot,' said Lionel.

'I suppose, but if you were there ...' She was flirting. It wounded me but the pain felt good. It meant that I was not alone. If Sylvia had flirted with me, it would have really hurt because I would have known it was all just a joke. But I am a third person, I told myself. Their happiness confirms the fact that I am lonely. Outwardly I am with them; inside, as usual, I am by myself.

I watched Lionel as he talked with her. He had a smile on his face which I had never seen before. He looked happy in a different way than he had before. In Debrakot there had always been a wistful anticipation in his eyes. It was not earnestness. It was a vacant stare. His eyes were like broken windows. Sylvia had made them come alive. He smirked, giggled, laughed, and his eyes never left her the whole evening. They seemed to reflect her brightness.

'I don't really like Delhi,' said Lionel. 'It's too rushed.'

'That's true,' said Sylvia sympathetically, though I knew she didn't understand.

They didn't even realize that I was sitting there. Maybe I looked as if I was thinking. They didn't want to bother me. Sylvia would never have gone so long without saying something to me or at me. She never spent so much attention on one person. Usually she juggled men around and kept all of us clutching to the edges of her conversation, each eager to say something. Tonight for the first time she was alone with someone. I was ignored, like furniture, an overstuffed sofa. The music banged against my skull. I stood up and went to the loo. They were in the middle of the floor. The band was setting up. One of the guitarists was playing alone with the record. I went back to our table and ordered another lime soda. When the waiter brought it I asked him for a piece of paper and a pencil. Lionel and Sylvia were still dancing and didn't seem ready to stop. I wrote them a note and left it under the ashtray on the table.

Outside, the night seemed limitless. I felt as if I could see farther in the darkness than I could during the day. A remorseless feeling of loneliness came over me. I tried to stop it but it seemed to tear into me, clawing at my body. Every inch of flesh crawled with the sensation, ripping me apart to the bone, shredding tendons, nodes, glands, fat. Talons sank into my soft muscles. I felt like a shellfish being pried out of its armour. There were no bones in me. I was loose and watery, like jelly. I was a glutinous organism like the ones found under decaying logs or old boards. There was nothing to me. I was a parasite, wrapping myself around people and sticking to them, a glutton, a gorged leech. I had sagging breasts. Pain skewered them like oysters on a fork. My thighs seemed to be pierced in a hundred places. My own hands clutched at my throat and dug into the loose skin with terror. I seemed afraid of a monster but the night and the streets were empty. I felt as if I was held in the embrace of an obese and grimacing giant. Then I realized it was myself. I was folded around myself. I was both the captor and the captive.

All the way home in the scooter rickshaw I thought about losing weight. How had I let myself become like this? I could still remember very clearly being thin, a boy running across a playing field chasing a football, swimming in streams, wrestling, climbing trees. I remembered laughing at the other boys who were overweight and chubby, who couldn't join in games. The only thing I couldn't remember was getting fat. It seemed to have happened overnight. I have always blamed my grandmother and I still know it was her. She fed me constantly. But there was a time before I was fat and a time afterwards, nothing in between. It couldn't have happened overnight.

The next morning I stayed in bed until twelve. Karim brought me tea and toast at about eight-thirty and I lay with my head propped up on a pillow for the next three hours plotting my strategy. It would be a perfect plan. I would get thin as quickly as I seemed to have got fat. Nobody but Karim would witness the transition. Alone in my room I would peel off my extra weight. It would be like undressing. And in the end, I would emerge slender and athletic. Of course, Karim would have to go to the tailor and have a new, trim suit made for my re-entry into the world.

I called Karim into the room and told him to shut the door.

'Promise me,' I said, 'that you will help.'

'In what?' he asked, grinning.

'I am going to lose weight,' I said.

Karim giggled with embarrassment.

'I am going on a strict diet and exercise schedule from this minute on and you will make sure that I stick to my word.'

'Yes, Salim Sahib, whatever you say.'

'No, from now on you do not do what I say. You're no longer my servant. You're my trainer. If it takes locking me in this room without food, then do it.'

'But you will starve,' he said.

'That's the idea.'

'Sahib . . . the guest, the young man who came down with you?'

'Tell him I am sick. Is he up yet?'

'Yes, I just gave him his tea. He stayed out very late last night.'

'Go right now and tell him that I am sick and that he shouldn't bother me; I want to rest. Tell him that he is welcome to everything in the house and that Jhandah Singh can drive him anywhere he wishes to go. Now, go tell him and come back immediately. Also, bring the scales from my mother's bathroom.'

Karim gave me a puzzled look and then left the room. I got out of bed and shut the windows, pulled the drapes across, and made the room completely dark. On one side of the room there was a full-length mirror set into a bureau. In front of this I lit a candle. I took a floor mat and spread it in front of the mirror. Then I stripped to my undershorts and stood completely still, watching my image, a final glimpse of what I had been. I tried to imagine what I was going to look like when I lost all of the weight. My skin looked smooth and oiled in the candlelight. The soft light cast dull shadows where the folds of fat dimpled and overlapped. It seemed as if I had no hair on my body, as if I was made out of plastic or wax.

When Karim returned with the scales, I weighed myself. I was just over two hundred pounds. Karim shaved me and then took a bottle of coconut oil from the top of my dresser. I lay down on the mat in front of the mirror and let Karim massage the oil into my skin. The pores seemed to soak it up. After a little while as Karim's hands increased their pressure it felt as if the fat was oozing out of me. I let him twist every muscle and tendon to the breaking point. It felt as if he was wringing the fat out of me. When he was through,

I did some exercises, as many as I could until my head began to feel dizzy. It had been a long time since I'd done them. I did push-ups, knee bends, and a few sit-ups. Every time I started turning red in the face and wheezing, Karim would grab me and make me stop.

'Slowly, Salim Sahib, slowly. Do not strain yourself,' he said. 'I will press your muscles again.'

The sweat rolling down my arms and back mixed with the coconut oil. It felt slimy. Karim's hands were sweaty and seemed to glide over my skin. He relaxed the muscles I had tightened with my exercises and gradually the aches dissolved.

'What did Lionel say?'

'Oh, he said it was too bad that you were sick and that he would see you this evening. He is going swimming today, at Maiden's Hotel.'

'Did he say with whom?'

'No, Salim Sahib, he did not. Are you thirsty? I will get you a Coca-Cola.'

'Yes,' I said, 'with plenty of ice.' The room felt very warm and the sweat dripped off my forehead into my eyes. I kept wiping it with my hands and soon my face was covered with coconut oil. I looked into the mirror. My body shone in the muted light.

I was alone in the room, in the mirror, in myself. Even Karim was gone. The dark walls on four sides of me were blank. The only face staring at me was my own. I stretched my arms above my head and watched the folds of fat around my waist disappear. Alone, I could be anyone I wanted. Outside of the room was a world of narrow, scrawny people. What made my size an oddity? Maybe they were all odd and I was normal. I dropped my arms to my side and the flabby contours dropped into place. For the first time I liked the seclusion of my room. On any other day I would have got bored and run outside to find someone.

By teatime I had done three sets of exercises, each one a little slower and more painful than the first. In between Karim loosened the knots and relaxed me. The room smelled stale with sweat and coconut oil. The air seemed dense and almost milky. I could tell that Karim was tired. He stopped two or three times to rub cramps out of the palms of his hands.

'It is time for tea, Sahib. I will bring you a tray up here.'

I was hungry but I told him, 'No, I won't have any. Go and get a cup for yourself. Drink it in the kitchen and then come back. The cook will give you something to eat as well.'

Karim jumped up and scuttled out the door. I rolled over on my back. My stomach was still there, thrusting up in front of me. Four hours had gone by since I had started my fast and already I was wanting to quit. As I lay there I told myself that the best thing would be not to think about it, but what else was there to think about?

Sylvia and Lionel would be at Maiden's now, swimming, sitting together under an umbrella, drinking Fanta and eating chips. I wanted to be there, not because of them, but because I could order a snack. It was still hard to believe that she could have fallen for him. He was not particularly handsome, not masculine by any means. Maybe she liked him because he was so shy. All of us were loud and rowdy. So was Sylvia, but maybe Lionel's quiet manner and polite voice soothed her. Maybe he was just stealthy like a cat. Was I jealous? No, I felt as if I had just paired two cards in my hand and put them down on the table. With that trick, I lost everything.

If they put me into a vacuum jar and pumped it full of pressure, how long would it take for me to shrink? I would feel it grip my arms like wet clothes at first and then tighter and tighter, gripping me all around like a vice. The meat and fat would be compressed into a hard, tight body. I would be taut and slim. My shirt would cover me like a tent. My trousers would slip over my hips and fall to the ground . . .

That night I suffered. I refused dinner even though my stomach moaned like a hollow conch shell. Karim brought me plenty to drink, so that I sat and sweated most of the evening. I went to bed early but couldn't fall asleep. I suffered until about one o'clock, when Lionel came in. I heard Karim open the door for him. There was a short conversation and then he came upstairs. My door opened a crack and he peered in. I pretended to be asleep.

I woke at about four-thirty in the morning, climbing all over myself with hunger. Nothing could hold me back. I went downstairs to the kitchen and ate an entire bunch of bananas and most of a loaf of bread. Karim, whose bed was in the hall, woke up at the sound of me eating and came in to watch. We said nothing to each other but he followed me back up the stairs half an hour later and began massaging my back again.

The fast was over and I ordered a huge meal when the cook came in. I tried not to think about it and just ate, quickly and without tasting the food. Karim brought me things to eat all day. I didn't want to leave the room. I wanted to remain alone. The room felt secure and Karim seemed to be the only person I could trust.

Lionel knocked on my door sometime in the morning but I told Karim to tell him to go away.

'Shall I get a doctor for you?' Lionel shouted from outside the door.

'No, it's all right. I'll be okay in a few days. How's Sylvia?'

There was a pause. 'Good,' he said. 'We're going out to dinner tonight.'

I didn't say anything more and after a few minutes Lionel seemed to have left.

A skilled doctor might be able to operate on me. They say that some surgeons can remove fat from a person's body. They could skin me completely, all over, and then peel away the extra weight, the white layers around my arms and legs. They could cut it off in strips and then sew me back up again. The seams might show . . .

For the next two days I didn't move any farther than from the mat on the floor to my bed. The candle in front of the mirror was kept lit and when it burned down to a drooping stub, Karim replaced it. We didn't talk very much. Karim would watch me eat and then take away the plates. He did not share my meals with me but must have fed himself in the kitchen. Karim was constantly massaging me. He would stop sometimes and shake his hands at the wrists, loosely like tassels, until the cramps went away. Once or twice he had to stop for half an hour. Not once did he ask me when I was going to leave the room. He did not complain but stayed with me faithfully. His hands were the only company I had and after a while they began to feel almost a part of me.

If I heated the room to high enough a temperature it would work like an oven and all of the fat could bake off of me. I could hang from a bar in the middle of the room and let the grease drip onto the floor. In between they would take me down and marinate me until the meat fell off my bones. In a day or two I would be thin . . .

'Karim,' I said. It was the fifth day in the room. 'Help me move the bed over to that side of the room.'

The two of us dragged the heavy wooden frame across the floor. There was a square of dust where it had stood before.

'Now, the dressing table goes next to it. The bureau can stay where it is. No, just a minute ...' I shut my eyes and tried to picture my grandmother's room. 'It stood right at the foot of the bed. In the middle of the room. There wasn't any desk but there were trunks in the corner covered with shawls and rugs. Put a blanket over the desk. There was another mirror in her room. It used to watch me from the wall directly in front of the bed. I would stare at it when I got bored. Get the round one, Karim, from my mother's dressing room and also have the cook make some pakoras and order some sweets from the Bengali sweet house. Tell him that I want two or three kilos. Go now, and come back quickly.'

I rushed around the room clearing things up and rearranging minor details. The room was a little larger but with the drapes pulled it had the same atmosphere. It almost smelled like her room, that rich odour, like moss or loam. To an outsider coming into the room it would have been a foul smell but to me it was a thick, sweet aroma, full of security.

When Karim came back, he brought a box of biscuits with him. We sat on my bed and ate them. At first he was shy but I made him take them. He was like a wild animal being hand-fed. His tiny fingers would grab at a biscuit and then he would turn his head and eat it privately but always with one eye on my face. Slowly he relaxed and when the biscuits were finished I sent him down to the kitchen again to get the pakoras. We ate them more slowly. I dipped the first one in a puddle of ketchup and held it up to Karim's mouth. His lips slowly opened and I pushed it between them. The ketchup dripped onto his chin. As we finished the pakoras, Karim began to refuse my offerings. He said that he was full but I made him eat them, saying that if he didn't I would be offended.

The sweets were packed in a square box. We each had a cup of tea first and then began eating them row by row. There were four pieces of pink coconut barfi. We each had two pieces. There was candied squash and pumpkin, so sweet that it made our teeth itch. Karim shook his head when I gave him one. It was saturated with syrup and he had to take it into his mouth because it was dripping on his clothes. I laughed at the way he bulged his cheeks as he chewed it. I ate a few pieces of pastry and made Karim take some shandesh.

'You must eat as much as I do,' I said. 'That's the game.'

'Sahib, I cannot,' he said, rolling his eyes and smiling.

My stomach answered him with a gruff, thundering sound. We both giggled and I put both my hands to my belly. I remembered my grandmother's story.

'It's a tiger inside me,' I said.

Karim laughed and consented to a couple more laddus.

'Go and get some Coca-Cola,' I said. He rushed off gladly as if I had just freed him from prison.

I ate two or three more sweets and then fell onto my back and stared at the ceiling.

My grandmother was lonely both within herself and without. There was no tiger inside her belly. It was a big, empty cavernous space which she was always trying to fill up. In there it was lonely. It was as empty as this room and the noises were nothing but hollow echoes, swelling up inside her. She knew nothing but loneliness, within herself, within her room, and even outside the house, shrouded in her black bourka – a moving secret, a trapped memory.

When she died she gave me her body. I must live in the same loneliness she lived in. It was after she died that I really grew fat. I couldn't escape it. When I realized the fact, I grew determined to live with it. I rolled over and looked at myself in the mirror. Given my body, I would try to do the best I could to escape its prison.

When Karim returned, I sent him away. I drank one of the Coca-Colas and ate a few more sweets. In a few minutes I fell asleep.

With the blinds drawn, I had forgotten what time of day it was. When I woke, I went to the window and looked out. It was mid-morning. Outside, it was bright and my eyes stung from the sudden exposure. I dressed and went downstairs.

'Where is Lionel?' I asked the cook.

'He left, Salim Sahib, yesterday morning.'

'Did he say anything?'

'Nothing, Sahib,' said the cook.

I went upstairs and showered. The water ran off my skin as if I was made of butter. For six days the coconut oil had seemed to be a part of my skin. I scoured it off with a brush until my body was raw.

A week and a half later Lionel wrote me a letter:

Dear Salim,

Forgive me for not writing sooner but I have been busy with the orchard. You're lucky the hotel burned down. I only wish these trees would go up in flames.

What happened to you? Are you over your illness? Was it physical or psychological? Forgive me, but it seemed as if you didn't want to see me once we got to Delhi. I didn't understand the note you left under the ashtray at the Cellar. I hope I didn't offend you. Thanks for letting me stay at your house even though you were sick. I appreciated having Jhandah Singh and the car. It made things so much easier. Delhi was not as awful as I had expected but it is still nice to be back in Debrakot.

When I left, I thought of leaving you a note but there didn't seem to be terribly much to say. I hope you are not cross with me for taking off after Sylvia. We are madly in love, as they say in the movies. In fact – you're the first person I'm telling this to – she and I are going to get married in two months. Please tell her as much as you can about Debrakot, so that she will be prepared for coming here. Try not to frighten her away. I know you won't. You must come for the wedding.

By the way, I went up to the hotel yesterday to look around. The only thing that I could find that I recognized was the old car in the shed. It's completely charred and mangled. It was a shame that it was destroyed before the road came up to rescue it. Too bad, I had visions of the two of us riding down to Jamshedpur in it. The road seems less sinister to me now, with Sylvia coming. Debrakot needs to open up to the plains, somewhat. But it will always remain somehow isolated and remote.

Sincerely,

Lionel

I read the letter over twice and put it in my pocket. Sylvia was probably at home and I decided to go congratulate her right away. I felt relieved about everything and I watched the buildings peel off the windows of the car as Jhandah Singh sped me across town. I would never go back to Debrakot. But to celebrate their wedding, I told myself, I will go to the Khyber that day and have a huge feast.

SIX . *Violation*

'Put the point of your knife just below the anus. Push the blade under the skin and slit it open all the way up to the neck. Be careful not to push the point in too far; the belly might pop and you will have to step back a few minutes to let the smell disperse.

'What's wrong? You can't have a weak stomach and be a hunter. Skinning the animal is part of a process, Lionel, just like anything else. The enjoyment in hunting lies in completing that process accurately and thoroughly. That's why men enjoy it more than women. A woman is scattered and undisciplined, whereas a man must have his rituals in order to be completely happy. He is systematic. The hunt is a ritual. It has been passed down from the earliest men, who killed with wooden clubs and stones. They began the rituals we follow now. They prepared themselves for the hunt, made weapons, stalked game, killed, skinned, butchered, and ate it.

'You hunted the goat and killed it. You carried it back here and now you have to finish the process. Don't puke like a woman just because there's a lot of blood.

'Yes, that's right; start a bit lower perhaps. Are you sure the knife is sharp?

'One fellow I used to hunt with never carried out the whole ritual. He was an American missionary, C. T. Ober. We went on two or three shikars together. I never liked him, though; he was sullen and wouldn't drink even when he was away from his wife. When he went hunting he always took along four boys. One carried his rifle; one lugged his thermos and a wicker basket full of sandwiches; one had good eyesight and spotted for him. The fourth would retrieve the animal and skin it. All Ober did was kill. God, he was a sour bastard. He couldn't have enjoyed the hunting.

'Good, you didn't burst the stomach. Now, carry on right up the breastbone, not too high, though, it will ruin the cape. What's wrong with you, Lionel, your hand's shaking? Do you feel sorry for the poor thing? Don't start crying.

'You're ready to gut it. Start on the belly. Here, I'll hold its legs apart.

'I'm too old to hunt and I realize it. I could still kill an animal but it wouldn't please me as much. Until I was fifty I did everything myself.

'Go ahead, work your fingers under the skin, just as if you were putting your hands up a girl's dress. You have to do it slowly. Don't look so serious. Just think of that girl in Lucknow. You'll have to go a lot deeper than that. Get up higher there. Okay, here comes the belly. Let me get behind and tip the whole thing up. All right now, reach way in. You're bound to get blood on yourself sometime, so don't worry about it. Do you feel the lungs? You're not high enough. Pull the entrails out first. Now, just slit the diaphragm. Have you got it? Good, just cut the whole mess of tubes in there. Sooner or later you'll hit the right one. Watch it! Keep those legs apart. Don't get blood on the skin. See, suddenly all of it lets loose like that. Cut off the liver and kidneys. The heart is still in there. Be careful, that's the gall bladder there, don't pop it.

'Part of the fun is getting bloody. You have to get your hands in among the juices and guts. Play with the mess, as if you were a little boy in the mud. Until your fingers go inside and touch an animal's heart, you won't believe you've killed it. It's like Thomas putting his hand in the wound or touching a woman to make sure she's there. You have to get the blood on you.

'Cut the gall bladder off.

'I know one fellow that always swallows the gall bladder when he skins an animal. He says it gives him strength, which I doubt. The bile is bitter enough to kill a man but it's part of his ritual.

'Wait a minute. That always happens. Don't start until I tell you. Try to cut in a straight line, right up the inside of the leg. The blade will slip around but keep it on the inside as much as possible. Otherwise it will mess up the skin.

'I enjoy this part of the skinning the most. Work your thumb in there. It always reminds me of peeling a pomalo, the way the skin comes off crisply like that. Now use your fist. You can't be gentle. I don't think you're going to need a knife now, except to cut the neck.

'The last part of the process is telling stories. That's all I'm good for now. I'd help you with this but you've got to learn, and besides, I'm old and not as able any more.

'You should see what it's like skinning an elephant. Actually, you never really skin it. It's chopped up – takes all day. There was a rogue at Lal Dhang shooting block one time. I went with a shikar party. Two of us shot it together. It charged and we put eight .458 bullets into its forehead before the damn thing dropped. The best fun was watching them gut it. The fellow who shot it with me had been in East Africa and told us that people there ate the meat. He got a few villagers to cut it open, partly to show the rest of us how big its stomach was and also because he had three dogs and he said that we could feed them the meat. The dogs liked it even though they were sick afterwards. But, Lionel, you should have seen those poor villagers cutting it up. They took all their clothes off and climbed right inside.

'You're ready to cut the neck now. Let me hold it for you. There's going to be a lot of blood. Cut slowly. When you get most of the neck severed, then we can twist it and break the vertebrae.

'Anyway, you should have seen those men when they came out of that elephant. They were covered with blood, painted with it. The three dogs got inside also and we had to wash them off in the canal . . .'

I dropped the knife and stood up. Holding my hands away from myself, I ran to the water pump. The Brigadier shouted something after me but I didn't listen. I wanted to get the blood off of my hands. I wanted to get away from the goat I'd shot. But most of all, I wanted to get away from the Brigadier with his instructions, his hoarse voice, his stories. The water gushed out of the pump. I began to rinse my hands. I scrubbed at them but the stains remained in the creases of my knuckles and under my fingernails. I took a handful of gravel and rubbed it between my palms and all over the backs of my hands until they stung. The water collected in pools around the pump. There were red swirls of blood in some of the puddles. My reflections looked up at me out of each of them. I pulled myself erect and began to walk away from the bungalow and the pump.

We were in the foothills below Debrakot. The bungalow stood on a dry meadow, bounded on one side by a river bed of round boulders through which a thin stream slipped down the valley, like a shiny green snake. Behind the bungalow, where I was standing, rose a natural fence of bamboo thickets holding back the tangled jungle. On all sides the red dirt ridges stretched up the mountain, gashed by landslides. Far above us the ranges of forested peaks reached up and back into each other like layers of shadow.

This was not my first hunting trip. I had gone with my father a number of times. But from the beginning, from the Brigadier's first mention of the trip until the shots which brought my goat cartwheeling down the mud cliff, I had felt helpless and uncertain of what I was doing. The brutality of the hunt had shocked me. It had been calculated, a ritual. The Brigadier seemed to be testing me, manipulating me. He had been beside me when I shot, whispering instructions in my ear, telling me exactly where to aim.

The sound of the rifle was crisp and I heard the bullet whine past me almost before the report. Turning quickly, I saw the Brigadier standing by the bungalow. He was working the bolt of his rifle. I stood still only long enough to see him raising the gun to his shoulder. Another shot exploded behind me. One of the stalks of bamboo about a foot away splintered. Before the next shot I was inside the jungle, crouching behind a lantana bush. The Brigadier moved towards me with the rifle still tucked into his shoulder.

'What's wrong, are you scared of blood? Are you a coward, Lionel?' the Brigadier shouted. Each word burst through the air at me. I held myself still and watched him stalk towards me.

Latif was asleep in the chaukidar's quarters on the other side of the bungalow. The chaukidar called out from his window.

'What is it, sahib ji?'

'Shut up, you bloody fool,' said the Brigadier. 'It's a peahen and you've scared it away.' To emphasize what he had said, he fired another shot into the bamboo. The chaukidar kept silent. The

Brigadier stopped at the place where I had been standing and scanned the ground for blood. It was a frightening gesture that made my nerves twitch.

I tried to move as quietly as I could but he heard me as I pushed my way through the lantana. He fired in the direction of my noise and then I heard him breaking his way into the jungle. He was too old to hunt. He had said so himself. I easily escaped him, running down a rough game track which took me farther and farther into the jungle. I finally stopped at a wide point in one of the valleys, dropping behind a cluster of boulders from where I could watch the path.

Up until that moment I did not think. I was like a scared animal racing away from the bullets and the shouting man. My feelings had all been wild and uncontrolled, completely irrational. Escape was the only thought in my mind, a driving, urgent force which hurled me through the forest.

It was the warm part of the day, just after noon. There was a humid lull permeating the forest. A coppersmith, hidden from sight, softly called, its voice like the sound of a hammer beating metal. It set the tempo for the forest and nothing moved except in time to its lazy beat.

Crouched behind the boulders, my knees sinking into the damp earth, I could not believe that the Brigadier was after me. It seemed more like a game, a chase through a childhood world. I thought of my brother Tony, hiding somewhere in my parents' garden, pursued by an imaginary enemy, a lion or a soldier. It was always at this time of day, when lunch was over, you felt like jumping and running around the house, like a bomber pilot or a screaming railway engine gone berserk. But for everyone else it was nap time and children were told to keep quiet. I always wanted to clamber up the bougainvillaea to the top of the roof and rage at the world, or climb a tree and go hand over hand through the branches, hooting in fluent monkey. My father would grab me and send me whimpering into hiding with a few swift blows from the palm of his hand.

Where was Tony? I knew the garden well and could picture every detail. He could be behind the jasmine bush or under the grapefruit trees. Then I saw him lying flat on his belly behind the compost heap, eyeing my parents suspiciously. He eased himself onto his hands and knees and scuttled a few yards ahead, dropping behind the hedge, from where he could secretly reach the Chinese oranges, which were sour and made you grin. He was a commando chasing the Japanese in Burma, a wounded officer escaping the Germans deep in their own territory, an agent carrying orders through enemy lines. My parents were always the enemy, the alert or sleeping guards, ready to pounce on you at any moment. If they caught you they would beat you to death with the palms of their hands. I remember watching my father's eyelids drooping as he fell asleep and waiting behind the lettuce patch near the castor trees for him to nod and begin snoring so that I could run across the open yard and take cover in the jungle of hollyhocks.

I could see my parents clearly, as if they were in front of me. Mother is gardening. She uses her hands instead of her mind. When she is angry they clench into fists, then tighten, they flail the air, they have expressions like a face. As my father grows old he becomes less important. He seems to fade with each year. There seems to be less and less to talk with him about. He is nothing but a blur. They are both ageing, one furiously and in a tantrum and the other patiently like a flower drooping.

I wished Tony was with me now. He could have helped me escape the Brigadier. Together we were great strategists and could have outwitted Rommel in the desert. It was always Tony and I against our parents. We were a pair of conspirators, plotting our escape from the garden world.

As I sat in the damp earth, the panic flowed out of me. It had struck me brutally, without time to think. The instincts settled, the fear softened until it was no longer fear but a malleable and understandable idea. I held myself back and tried to realize what had happened.

It was not Tony's and my world. It was the Brigadier's. He had gone mad. The shots had been real but everything else was make-believe. It was all in the Brigadier's mind. Where was he? I wondered. He was not there in the foothills. Who did he think he was? What part was I supposed to play? I was not myself. All that mattered was who he thought I was. It made me angry to have him turn me into someone I didn't want to be. He was using me.

In Debrakot people lived in a world of imaginary things. It was a town outside of India, separated from what really happened. The Brigadier and his wife wrapped themselves in fictions. Mrs Augden would probably be on her porch now, knitting or reading the teen-age novels she so enjoyed. From where she sat, these ridges were probably visible, far below her like wrinkled fabric.

She lived with the Brigadier as if she was his spinster sister rather than his wife. I think she sometimes imagined I was her lover. That is an embarrassing thing to say about a sixty-year-old woman, but I felt it. She had a mothballed sensuality, which was preserved under her ageing features. Once in her room she lifted the hem of her dress up her thigh to show me a bruise she had got the day before. She held the dress up a few moments longer than was necessary, and I felt her desire strongly, listening to her breathless chatter.

When I came to Debrakot the Brigadier greeted me warmly, the son of his best friend. I was to live in his house, eat his food. We didn't talk often, though he did open up with drink. He said he was the same age as my father but he seemed twenty years older. His body must have been stocky and powerful at one time but it had collapsed on him now.

I had come to Debrakot to take over his orchard. I didn't take over, instead he continued running the place with me as his assistant. I was shown only what he wanted to show me. He kept his secrets and loved to make me stumble over something he hadn't explained. When I made mistakes he would tell me that he wasn't sure I could handle the job. He was worried that it would be too much for me.

I learned not to get in his way. It didn't bother me except when he shouted at me for his own mistakes. I let him run everything and just joined in as his junior associate rather than an heir. My father had made some business transaction with the Brigadier but it had gone on above my head and all I knew was that my place was secure. It had almost seemed as if my father had sold me as a foster son.

I saw nothing in him that reminded me of my father. How could they have been friends? What made even less sense was that my father had sent me to him. Of course, there had been the trouble with Sujeeta in Lucknow. I couldn't stay there after that got around. But there was more to my coming to Debrakot than just to escape a scandal.

I decided to climb the ridge and get a view of the valley. There was a rock jutting out of the ridge about a hundred yards above me.

From there I would be able to spot the Brigadier and still remain safe. I had begun to believe my imagination. Fear takes games and turns them into reality. Lies come true, like dreams.

Scrambling up the slope, pushing my way through thorn bushes and patches of high grass, I kept myself in some sort of cover all the way to the rock. The trees had suddenly come alive with birds, magpies and laughing thrushes all hooting and whistling at me. I felt sure they were going to betray me to the Brigadier and waited for the moment when a bullet would come crashing into my back and slam me crumpled in the dirt. There was no shot and it was only after I had been squatting on the overhanging rock for half an hour that the Brigadier appeared around a bend in the ravine. He was walking slowly, with a slight limp, and he stooped down every couple of minutes to check my spoor. The ground was muddy and my tracks must have shown up clearly. He followed my trail, ducking in and out of sight behind trees and clumps of bamboo. At one point he looked directly up at where I was sitting. The sun was behind me and I kept still, so that he didn't pick me out. His eyes were bad anyway.

He said they had been damaged by the hours he had spent exposed to the bright sun in the desert. He had fought in the Sahara with an armoured division and once in a while told stories about the war. They were horrible stories about the heat and dehydration, made even more horrible by the way the Brigadier told them. It was probably the only way he could live with those stories, if they were true. He told them like jokes. Each one had its punch line.

I never wanted to hear the stories but he would force them on me. One in particular I remember. It was about a young Muslim captain who was a gunner in a tank. It was his first major action. They were accompanying a division of British tanks. The German attack outnumbered the British and the young Muslim's tank was called in with the others to help out. He was afraid and didn't want his body burned if the tank blew up. It was superstition but he opened the hatch so that in case they were hit he could jump out. A German soldier happened to notice the open hatch and tossed a grenade inside. The Brigadier told the story with a straight face up until then; after the last line he burst out laughing and snickered to himself the rest of the evening.

It made me cringe. I felt horror, the same way I had felt when his wife lifted her dress in front of me. These people were grotesque. It was like cracking open an egg and finding an embryo, except that I was the embryo.

Was he going to skin me after he had hunted me down and put a bullet through my head? I could stay away from him forever, lead him far into the jungle and then back-track, pick up my things at the bungalow, and leave. I watched him moving in deliberate circles up and down the valley, catching my trail and then losing it. His madness gave him determination. He would die before he let me get away. He may have missed the first time but when he found me next the sights would be dead on my heart. He would tighten his finger on the trigger. All of my sensations would rush in a burning spear of pain to where the slug tore its hole in my skin and ripped aside the flesh to get at my heart. The bleeding would flood inside of me. I'd jump and land on my back, roll off the rock, and crash down through the branches until a thorn bush or a tree trunk stopped me. The Brigadier would pull me out into an open glen and strap me onto his back to take back to the bungalow . . .

Perhaps the sun had done more than just ruin his eyes. Maybe the desert had driven him mad. Where did he think he was? In Egypt, lost in the Sahara, following the tracks of a dangerous Nazi general? Did my bootprints seem to leave crooked swastikas in the mud? I pictured his world. It was a hot dry day, the air like yellow cellophane, mirages and heat waves massing and dispersing on the horizon like an enemy. Through the hushed and endless sand, a man came tracking after me. There was nowhere to hide. I ran on over the shallow dunes, lying flat sometimes and stretching my eyes along the hem of the sky. I caught sight of him among the shimmering mirages. There was no wind to erase my footprints. Where they sank into the sand they remained, impressions of my fear. Suddenly ahead of me loomed the geometric shape of a pyramid. I began to run towards it, lunging forward through the sand, which yanked at my ankles. I reached the first steps and pulled myself quickly to the top. From there I could see for a great distance and the Brigadier was only a dot, a speck of black like a beetle on the sheets of sand. As he moved towards me he grew bigger. Then suddenly with him there were dozens of tanks grinding towards me. I huddled behind the pyramid . . .

At the bungalow, the Brigadier sharpened his knife on a smooth stone from the river bed. He made the first incision a few inches below my navel. The knife slid under my skin and opened me up to the throat. I could feel nothing but see it all. He gutted me quickly, without effort. My heart had been shattered and there was a great deal of blood. He peeled the skin back, down my sides, and then cut along the legs. My skin slit easily. He dismembered me limb by limb and I felt nothing even when he twisted my neck and broke the spine.

Could I have shattered the Brigadier's world, which had been so delicately constructed out of years of waiting? Waiting for what? A son perhaps – me? Though I was what he had wanted most of all, I was also threatening him. I was the signal for his retirement. I was another man in his family. Perhaps I reminded him of my father. He may have searched me for an image of himself and not found it. A father must always recognize himself in his son. More than anything, though, the Brigadier did not want to let go of his world, his bungalow, his orchard, Debrakot. It was a sterile, dying world.

We only quarrelled once – in the open. Some of the fruit pickers, low-caste men from the villages in the hills, tried to get out of work one day because there was a festival at the cobra temple, three miles west of Debrakot. The fruit was already too ripe on the branches and if it wasn't all picked within a week, most of it would spoil. The men asked to be allowed one day off and promised that they would work overtime the next few days.

The argument took place on the veranda of the bungalow. We had been having tea. The hill men came nervously up the path towards us, the oldest of them stooped partly with age and partly with respect. They were all dark men, wearing nothing above their waists. The sweat shone on their foreheads and ran rivulets through the dust on their bodies.

'Speak up, bloody!' said the Brigadier to the old man's mumbled apology.

The old man explained their request. The Brigadier started to get angry. At first I hated him for what he was doing and then I hated the pickers for being so frightened of him. When I spoke it came out of me without my trying to say anything. I took the side of the pickers.

The Brigadier went off his head and told me to get out of sight. I left him there, beet red in the face and calling the fruit pickers every dirty name there was. After he had finished with them he came back at me and almost hit me. 'Don't ever go against me in front of those bastards! Lionel, there's only one thing in this world that counts. It's sticking to your own side in any situation. As soon as you change sides you become one of them.' I tried to explain that to me it seemed a fair demand and that they could work at night if necessary. But the Brigadier grew more and more angry until I stopped arguing and went to my room. We spoke in monosyllables for a week or so until the fruit was off the trees.

Perhaps it was from that time on that the Brigadier hated me but I think it started earlier. There was a strange blood tie between us, maybe the Saxon in us. It was like being part of a family. Our Christianity, our English manners, our English pedigree, all linked us to each other. When we fought it was like a father and son, or an uncle and nephew fighting. There had always remained a bond between us. I realized my own relationship to the Brigadier, even though I was beginning to hate him. A hatred within a family is stronger than that outside of one.

Either the Brigadier or Mrs Augden is sterile. They have never had children. One of them must be, but it could be either. She is always nervous, like a spayed bitch. He is dull and sedentary, like a castrated dog. But there is always violence brewing beneath his surface. It doesn't matter now, I suppose, they are both beyond the age of having children.

The Brigadier was moving in wide circles. He had lost my trail and was trying to recover it. There was a methodical determination to the way he scouted all around the valley, moving in deliberate and widening circles, using a thicket of bamboo as his axis. It was fascinating to watch him. He had obviously been a good hunter in his day. The walls of his bungalow attested to that. They were covered with skins and trophies, each one with its own story – a long chase, tracking, danger, frustrations, but always, in the end, the well-directed shots which brought the animal down.

Mrs Augden had showed me some of her albums one afternoon. It was a few months after I had arrived. The Brigadier had gone to Jamshedpur on business and was to return late that night. I was reading in my room when she entered with the wide volumes under her arm. She spread them on my bed, telling me that she had meant to show them to me earlier. Patiently I waited as she flipped through the black pages pasted full of snapshots.

'There,' she said, opening the album to a page full of prints.

My mother and father grinned at me. They looked much younger than I ever remembered them, wearing fashions I thought had been and gone even before their time. One picture showed my father and the Brigadier dressed in bush jackets and jodhpurs with puttees and pith helmets. They were standing beside an elephant and held rifles in their hands. For a moment I remembered a picture the Brigadier had Latif snap of himself and me holding rifles in front of the bungalow. He posed the same way beside me, with his right leg forward and slightly bent, his eyes staring away from the camera.

Some of the photographs I remembered seeing around our house when I was young, in my mother's drawers or in silver frames on her dresser. They were windows on the black pages, looking back into an age when Charles, Millie, Teddy, and Nat were newly married and full of laughter. I thought of them now, my mother with her face wrinkled and dark like a raisin despite her lavender powder, my father old and silent, the grey creeping up to meet his receding hairline. Mrs Augden withered and sexless under her nightgown, showing me pictures when her husband was away, pressing herself against me as we gazed at the photographs. And the Brigadier, a militaristic march hare, bristling with blunt threats, but as harmless as a puffed-up toad.

The Brigadier was like a rogue elephant. Separated from the herd, he had gone mad. Had he hoped that I would accept him as a father, obey him, and attempt to follow his examples? I could only guess.

My squeamishness when I was skinning the goat must have set him off, or maybe he had plotted it out, bringing me on this hunting trip with the one motive of killing me. No, he was a rogue, a man gone mad. His confidence, his life had been shattered.

In the twilight I saw him climbing the ridge opposite me. It was not as high a ridge and there was a gradual game path which wound its way to the top. I waited until the old man had reached the top and then lay down flat on the rock. From there I yelled.

'Uncle!'

He twirled around to face me, pulling the rifle up to his shoulder. We were about two hundred yards away from each other. He didn't say anything.

'Why do you want to kill me?'

The rifle snapped to his cheek and he fired at nothing. The slug thudded into the dirt about twenty-five yards to my right. I was surprised how close it was but I knew that he didn't see me. I was hidden by the angle of the rock.

'Show yourself, coward!' His voice was hoarse and seemed to shatter in the air, each syllable hitting me like shrapnel.

'It's me, Lionel,' I shouted. 'Why do you want to kill me?'

'Bastard!'

'What have I done?'

He wasn't looking at me any more but gesturing over his shoulder frantically and giving orders to an imaginary army. 'Forward! He's up there on that ridge. Move the howitzers over to those trees. Range, two hundred yards even. Fire!' He shot again, this time below me.

There were more orders, most of them incoherent. He sent one party down the ridge to flush me out and then fired another round into the trees a hundred yards below me. The sky was dark and shadows were spilling over the ridges. His eyes must have been able only to see the dim outline of the ridge. I kept still, like a lizard on the rock. Half of his army was advanced up the valley to commence a flank attack on my position. There was a barrage of grenades and mortar fire over my head and then the Brigadier, with a sudden volley of shots, emptied the clip of his rifle and came running down the slope of the ridge. Before he had gone ten steps his legs tangled and he tumbled down the hillside, falling over boulders and bouncing against trees. He set off a landslide which partly buried him where he eventually stopped. I waited a few minutes, half expecting his army to lift him up and carry him away. He made no signs of moving, so I stood up and worked my way down to where he lay in the valley.

He seemed to be staring at something horrible and frightening. I tried to shut the lids of his eyes but they kept falling open on the terrified expression. He weighed more than I could carry. Maybe I should skin him, I thought to myself.

At the bungalow I told the chaukidar and Latif that he had fallen chasing peahens up the ridge. There was no reason to tell the truth. We lit torches out of pieces of wood dipped in pine sap. When the flames illuminated his face in the darkness, I looked at him carefully. He was not my father. And he knew it.

SEVEN . *The Motor Road*

Dear Sylvia,

Mrs Augden left today. She will be going to Kenya, where a brother of hers lives. The house is so empty. I am master of the place and yet I feel sometimes as if it is a prison and I am condemned to stay here for life. There was a time when I wanted seclusion, to live alone and lonely, as a hermit. I don't know why. I used to feel as if I was the only person left in the world. I wanted to be a ghost and haunt this town. But now you are coming . . .

A road is being built to Debrakot and there will soon be buses and cars driving up here full of vacationers and tourists. There will soon be plenty for you to do. I don't begrudge them coming now. You'll be here with me and if we choose to ignore them we will. The town will never get too big and it will be full only during the summer months. As I'm writing I can hear the dynamite exploding around the ridge where they are cutting the road out of the cliffs. It will be a winding road with hairpin turns and zigzags. Shall we buy a car some day so that we can ride up and down the mountain? It should be a convertible so that we can race around the turns with the wind in our faces. It seems as if they are building the road for your arrival. But it won't be done by the time you get here. You'll have to come up in a dandie or on a horse. Even when the road is completed we should sometimes ride down the old walking path, just because it will be there despite the motor road.

Only another week and you'll be here.

I love you,

Lionel

Lionel can be very silly sometimes. When I got off the train at Jamshedpur all of the coolies were whispering my name. One of them asked me if I was 'Sylvia Missahib'. I nodded, a little afraid, never having seen the station before in my life. The coolies snatched up my luggage and darted out the platform gate. Lionel wasn't around. He had promised to be there. I walked over to the gate and surrendered my ticket to the collector, who eyed me suspiciously. Everyone on the platform seemed to know who I was. I wondered if something had happened to Lionel.

As I stepped outside the station, there was a long wheezing noise, like a shopkeeper blowing his nose. The bagpipes wailed. The flutes caught the reckless tune and carried it above the cacophony of trumpets, clarinets, and the low thud of the drum. Out from behind the band stepped Lionel. He carried a garland of marigolds, which he dropped over my neck.

'Sorry, I can't kiss you now,' he said. 'It would be a scandal.'

Five more garlands slipped over my head. I was introduced to a bevy of elderly Anglo-Indians, none of whose names I remembered at the time. Lionel pulled me into a waiting tonga. The old driver clucked his tongue and the horse set off, tearing a path through the crowd of onlookers. I felt horribly foreign. The faces looked at me viciously. Crows attack pigeons, I thought to myself. Our little cluster of Anglo-Indians amidst a mass of hostile faces. I didn't want to feel the way I did. There is nothing foreign about me. The old couples seemed used to it and were chattering away in English, saying things like 'How these Indians stare.' 'Don't they ever get bored?' I am dark enough to pass for an Indian but when I am in a group of my own people I feel as if I am as conspicuous as them. Lionel was ignoring the crowd. I felt like yelling at the whole group in Hindustani. But they would only laugh at my accent.

Some of the people applauded, some jeered. I hung on to Lionel's arm and stared at him. The smell of marigolds was overwhelming.

'You're not angry at me, are you? I just wanted you to arrive in style.'

'When is it safe to kiss?' I asked.

'Any time now,' he said, leaning over me. We kissed half a dozen times until I realized the old couples were following us in a string of tongas. Even at a distance I could see them smiling. The driver of our cart didn't turn his head but kept clucking his tongue. I couldn't tell whether he was urging the horse on or disapproving of us.

'Who are they?' I asked, pointing behind me.

'That's the entire population of Debrakot, or what's left of it.'

'What do you mean?'

'Those are the old girls and boys I warned you about, the gossip club. Don't worry, I know they'll like you. They need a celebration once in a while and I thought this would cheer them up. It's a lark for them.'

'You mean they came all the way down here just to meet me?'

'Yes, a sort of grand escort.'

'How sweet,' I said, not meaning that at all.

At the foot of the hill we left the tonga. A cluster of horses and dandies waited to carry our party up the hill. Lionel took me by the hand and led me to one of the dandies. The four men who were waiting beside it grinned foolishly.

'Can I ride a horse?' I asked.

Lionel frowned.

'Please,' I said. 'I feel guilty riding in this – like an old mem-sahib.'

'If you do, one of the men will have to ride in a dandie and that wouldn't work.'

I started to argue but one of the old ladies came up to me and told me that it was really very comfortable and that all I had to do was lean back and enjoy the view.

Looking at Lionel so that he knew I hated doing it, I climbed into the seat. There was no point in arguing. After all, this was my wedding procession.

At first the road was wide enough for Lionel to ride beside me. He talked quickly, apologizing and promising the whole thing would be over in a couple of hours when we reached Debrakot. When the road got narrower he led the way and our conversation dwindled to a few shouts back and forth. The coolies carried me silently up the hill, staring straight ahead. All I could hear was their breathing, which grew louder as the incline increased.

'There's the new road!' Lionel shouted.

I looked up at the ridge across from us and saw a thin line of exposed earth where the road had been cut. Rubble and rocks had been tossed down the hill so that every valley and ravine was clogged with debris. Along the road I could see parties of labourers working and relaxing. At one point a large boulder was pushed over the edge and crashed down to the stream at the bottom, shattering trees and dragging behind it a landslide of smaller rocks, like the tail of a comet.

We seemed to be entering a forgotten world. As our line of horses and dandies crested the ridge, I looked back and was surprised to see the plains so far away. It was hard to believe that the coolies had carried me up so quickly. The path now delved into a series of smaller valleys and ridges which ran like ribs down the main part of the hill. The trees were dark and the ground dappled with shadows. The coolies stopped at a spring to get a drink and rest. The men tied their horses and then helped the women out of their dandies. One of the men, an old tiger with bloodshot eyes and a frightening limp, came towards me to help me out of the dandie. I was on my feet in a shot but thanked him anyway. He seemed flustered and mumbled something about sprightly young girls. Lionel caught me from behind. I wanted to kiss him again but they were all watching. If only we could have been alone.

'If you want, Sylvia, you can ride my horse. I'll walk. The dandie can come up empty.'

'No, no,' I said. 'Don't be ridiculous. You can't walk.'

'I do it all the time. I should have let you ride from the bottom of the hill.'

He was acting so polite. It irritated me. I just wanted to take his hand and race up the path around the corner and kiss him. I couldn't even whisper it in his ear. They were all watching. The old couples were trying not to, hunched together as if in conference but not saying a word. The coolies knotted themselves around the spring, their eyes and teeth darting smiles at Lionel and me.

'Here you go, lass!' said the decrepit tiger who had tried to drag me out of the dandie. He thrust a flask into my hand. The old tiger helped me pour out a shot into a tin cup.

'Put it where it belongs,' he said. The brandy tasted metallic. Lionel refused a drink. An ostrich, dressed in silk and feathers, brought us a tin of biscuits.

When I refused she looked as if she was going to put her head in the sand. Lionel took two and forced one into my hand.

'Mrs Saunders makes these herself. They're marvellous,' he said.

I glared at him but couldn't say anything. The dry crumbs glued themselves to my teeth. There was a faint taste of chocolate. I looked away and tried to keep from gagging. The ostrich went back to her cluster. They seemed to be expecting us to do something.

I felt like one of those South American virgins who is married to the God. She is treated like a queen, fed the best food, dressed in jewels and finery, but in the end the priests put her to death so that she can join her lord.

I was being taken to the slaughter. At points I imagined throwing myself out of the dandie and rolling down the hill to escape. The horses, the sweating coolies, the dandies, the mountains all had the aura of ancient rites and superstition. Even Lionel seemed to be a part of the plot, the way he smiled with knowing smugness. About three quarters of the way up there was a traveller's shrine housing an anonymous idol bathed in vermilion. The coolies all stopped and bowed reverently. I thought, here goes, I'm finished for sure, these are my executioners. They are going to carry me up to the highest point on the mountain and then tip the dandie and tumble me over a cliff. But after bowing to the idol and asking me for a marigold from my garlands – I gave them an entire garland – to decorate the shrine, the coolies picked me up and we continued towards Debrakot. The first houses were visible, bathed in lemon sunshine.

Lionel rode ahead proudly. In Delhi he had been shy and gentle. Here he seemed to be a warlord. Was he taking me to his fort? Was I a new girl for his harem? In Delhi we had sat alone for hours, hours which had blown past me like neem leaves in a storm, a storm which I held captured inside of me. It was a hurricane and he was the eye of it, quiet, still, peaceful. I wanted to find my way through the storm to his place in the centre, where he stood untouched by the spinning winds and the rain which fell like lead pellets.

Whether we sat in a noisy discothèque or in the shadows behind my house in Delhi, there was always a silence surrounding us, which muffled everything but our voices. As I was carried up the hill, he seemed far away on his horse. The storm gathered inside of me again.

We rode through the main street of Debrakot. Nobody seemed to be living there. Most of the doors had chunky padlocks on them and boarded windows. A small boy raced out of an alley and then, seeing us, slithered up a drain pipe and perched on the roof like a monkey, watching us with wild curiosity. There was no one else. On the far side of the town, the party began to disintegrate. The friendly warthog and his wife shook my hand sincerely and said goodbye. Their cottage was tucked into the hill just below the road. The puffin and the mongoose, two elderly sisters with chewed furs around them, were the next to leave, followed by Father Christmas with his white beard and heavy build. That left the lame tiger and his mate the ostrich. We moved on and arrived at Lionel's house. It was the first thing that I liked about Debrakot, old and sturdy with a fresh coat of whitewash and the garden lusty with flowers, poppies, hibiscus, and marigolds. Lionel tethered the horses.

'Latif! A pot of tea!' Lionel shouted inside. The old Muslim ignored his order and came out to have a look at me. Lionel introduced us and Latif seemed ready to burst into laughter or tears, I couldn't tell which. George and Cynthia, the tiger and the ostrich, settled into the sofa together as if it was their regular seat.

'I'd like to wash. Which room is mine?' I asked.

Lionel looked flustered.

'Come,' he said. 'Excuse us,' to the Saunderses.

He led me through a curtain into a large room, obviously his.

'Darling, until we're married you'll stay with the Saunderses. They live just above us here in a beautiful house. We'll be together all the time, only we won't sleep together, that's all. It wouldn't be proper.'

'I never thought you'd ever say that.'

'What?'

'That something wasn't proper. Lionel, I want to be with you. We haven't had a moment alone yet; will we ever? I don't want to live with a lame tiger and an ostrich.'

'What did you call them?' he said, laughing. 'That's a good description but they're very nice.'

'Why can't I stay here with you?'

'The rumours would spread like mad.'

'Who cares?' I said.

'It'll only be a few weeks until we're married. Imagine what your parents would say if they got up here and found us already living together. Mine would throw a fit.'

I held him tightly and tried to keep from crying.

'Why does everyone have to come to our wedding? Why can't we be married right now and be done with it? Oh damn, kiss me at least.'

Tea was very solemn and uncomfortable. Our sentences were pinched with nervousness. Lionel forced the Saunderses to stay for dinner. We sat for what seemed like hours. Cynthia leafed backwards and forwards through an old copy of *Span*. I tried to do crossword puzzles in my head without a pencil but then began to forget and became frustrated. George and Lionel discussed arrangements for the wedding. It was scheduled two weeks from now. That was supposed to give me enough time to find out if I liked Debrakot. It had seemed like a good idea at first. If I was going to live here for the rest of my life, I'd better see what it was like. It would have been all right if tomorrow was the wedding or if I could at least wait in Lionel's house. Instead I was going to be cooped up in a fusty tiger's den with an ostrich to look after me. I knew that if I stayed there more than a night or two, I'd hate Debrakot for the rest of my life.

'Sylvia, when are your parents planning to arrive?'

'The end of next week. Friday, I think.'

'Someone will have to meet them. They'll stay here, of course.'

'What about your family?' I asked.

'They'll stay here also. It'll be fun; since the two families are being joined, they might as well live together for a few days.'

'It's you and I that are getting married, not them, remember.'

After a dangerous pause, George interrupted the silence.

'You know, we haven't had a wedding in Debrakot since 1951.'

'But plenty of funerals,' added Cynthia with a honk of laughter.

We all spoke our dawdling English, with the same accent. What we talked about didn't matter. We were speaking *our* language, our English. Right in the middle of some silly conversation with Mrs

Saunders I wanted to stop myself and begin shouting at her in Hindustani. Of course, she only spoke kitchen-Hindi and was probably proud that she couldn't understand Indians. I felt as if I was speaking a foreign language.

After dinner Lionel and I took a few moments alone on the veranda. But I was cross at him, and though I let him kiss me, I quickly let go of him and said that I was tired and wanted to get to sleep.

'Of course,' he said.

We went up to the Saunderses' house in a group. It was only a quarter mile and Lionel and Latif carried my baggage. Lionel and I said good night abruptly and he vanished with Latif into the shadows. George snapped on the lights in the living room. I felt as if I had stepped back a hundred years. All of the furniture was old and sagging. It was very crowded and there were dust covers on everything. Lace doilies and tablecloths peeked out from every corner like petticoats. In the centre of the room a bloated stove with an extended chimney dominated the room. Pictures crowded the walls along with hunting trophies and plaques. There was a bust of Curzon as a Roman senator perched on the mantelpiece.

It was so removed from Delhi. The hush was deathlike. I felt as if I was being buried with all these nostalgic trinkets around me – the remains of my heritage.

George darted over to a cabinet and took out a crystal decanter partly filled with sherry. The three of us had to have a glass. We toasted the wedding. I realized that they weren't going to let me go to sleep and allowed George to pour me a second glass, which he did eagerly.

'That's a girl,' he said. 'It'll be nice to have a woman take charge of that boy. He's a fine lad but needs to serve drinks with dinner.'

'George, what a thing to say!' His wife looked embarrassed.

'No, nothing wrong with saying it. A man's got a right to get thirsty. People shouldn't inflict their teetotalling on others. That's being a bit pushy, don't you think? Even if he doesn't drink, he should serve it to his friends.' Then he turned to me. 'But you're a sensible lass. Look at the way she downs that sherry. There's sure to be something flowing in that house from now on.'

I laughed and suddenly felt very much in love with Lionel.

'You know, George, I was remembering our marriage...' Cynthia started to say.

'It's the first time in twenty years you've done that, my chipmunk.' He pinched her arm.

'The night before we were married George's friends took him out carousing in Calcutta. He was in the merchant marine. They got him drunk.'

'Nothing unusual about that,' added George.

'Once he was completely out they dragged him to an old Chinaman who sold opium and did tattoos...'

'I'll tell her the story,' interrupted the tiger with a roar. 'Yes, I was drunk. Everything was blurred and watery like I was under the sea or something. All I remember is being held down and this Chinaman with a waxy yellow face that looked like a painted balloon kept poking my stomach. I didn't feel too much except a little sting once in a while. I could hear my chums laughing. They held me down tightly so I couldn't move. I was gone by the end of it and just remember waking up in a friend's bed.'

'Show Sylvia the tattoo!' squealed Mrs Saunders.

'No, that would be indecent. She's just a bride. Just a chipmunk.'

I said nothing, trying to figure out whether I was supposed to ask to see the mark or not. I hoped he wouldn't show it to me. Cynthia went around behind him and they fought like two children. She kept tugging at his shirt and giggling. He tried to push her hands away. They looked ridiculous. In the end she won, standing behind him, victoriously holding up his shirt and vest over his fleshy belly. He lifted his arms above him, like a convict. Both of them grinned. He looked like a cat that had rolled over to let me scratch its stomach. I had to move closer to inspect the tattoo. It had been overgrown by a jungle of grey hair. The skin was yellow and speckled. There was an ornate design, with animals and birds flocking around his navel. But in the centre, written neatly, was the name Suzy.

'When I saw that after I woke up the next morning I thought I was going to have to call the wedding off.'

'Fortunately, I'd seen his stomach before we got married – when we went swimming together, of course –' She laughed. 'So, I believed his story.'

'You did not. It took me three years to convince you that there wasn't a Suzy in my life.'

I stepped back from the tattooed stomach and stared at the old couple, trying to imagine what it must have looked like when he was young. I thought of Lionel. His skin was smooth and babylike. Would he have a tattoo in the morning?

My room was small but not as cluttered as the rest of the house. The bed was narrow.

'In the morning you'll get a lovely view of Lionel's house from this window,' said Cynthia.

It was built for the view, curving outwards, what some people call a bay window. When the Saunderses had finally left me, I undressed. I wondered if Lionel could see me. There was a faint light on in his bungalow. I didn't shut the curtains and stood naked in the window for a few minutes just in case he was watching. Then I went to bed.

Even with the two glasses of sherry, I couldn't fall asleep. Lying on my back, I tried to imagine the marriage. There would not be too many people here, just my parents and Lionel's. Some friends of mine from Delhi had promised to come but I doubted if they would show up. There was a church and a minister in the town. That was all Lionel had told me. We were not going on a honeymoon. That way Debrakot would always seem like a honeymoon.

Did I like Debrakot? Nobody had asked me yet, not even Lionel. Maybe he was afraid I'd say no. Maybe he didn't care if I did or not. I had answers lined up for the question even before I got here and saw what it was like. 'Oh, such a darling house, I'll love fixing it up. Can I redecorate, sweetheart?' – 'The hills are so beautiful. They have a spiritual atmosphere.' – 'Oh, there will be plenty to do: I'll never get bored. How could I?' They were sophisticated answers from a city girl in the country. I had to tinge them with a hint of boredom, so that I didn't sound too sincere.

For a moment I wondered if Lionel would sneak up to the house and knock at the window. He might have seen me standing in the window and taken it as a challenge. The thought excited me. I took my nightgown off in case he came, so that when I got up to open the window, he'd see that I'd been waiting for him.

Would I really like Debrakot? If a lot of people visited me it would be nice. Maybe I could start a garden or maybe even a dispensary for villagers. That was what I could do, a humanitarian project. It would keep me busy and do some good for the people. Lionel could get medicines for me and I could distribute them and do social work. I would turn one of the rooms of the bungalow into a dispensary and hang a picture of Gandhi over the door. That would draw people to me.

But that was the future and I was more worried about the next few weeks. From what Lionel had told me about his parents, I was scared to meet them. Not because they would be so different from mine but because they sounded just the same. Lionel was cynical and said they were debauched and had 'gone to seed'. I wouldn't trust myself to describe my own parents. I'm sure I've made up so many untruths about my mother and father. Lionel said he really wished his weren't coming to the wedding. I want to meet his young brother, though. Tony probably looks like Lionel did when he was small. I want to give him a kiss and make him blush. My parents will get along with Lionel's.

They try so hard to be English, it's pathetic. They used to make me put Marmite on my toast when I was small, even though I preferred molasses and cream. My mother used to make her own marmalade too, out of the Chinese oranges which grew on a tree in our yard. She was proud of it and used to say that it was more authentic than Chivers. But she used to put it in empty bottles of Chivers and if somebody commented it was passed off as the real thing. My mother raised me as her image of an English schoolgirl and used to slap me if I ever spoke Hindustani in the house.

I just hope she doesn't think I'm marrying beneath us. Lucknow is less sophisticated than Delhi, I'm sure. She could get very nasty.

There was a sound outside the window. I held perfectly still and waited for the knock. After a few seconds I decided he thought I was asleep. Yawning, I stretched and then sat up. There was still no sound. Maybe it wasn't him. Perhaps if I left the window open it would be more of an invitation. I had been cold with him when we said good night. He could have been scared. Climbing out of bed again, I went over to the window and jiggled the latch free and pushed the window open. The air was warm and gentle, as if someone was breathing all over me.

Back in bed, I returned to thinking about our parents. Would they leave right after the wedding? Probably not. They'd be too drunk and disorganized. I imagined our wedding night. After two weeks of separation, Lionel and I would finally be together. Our house would be full of people. I could picture us lying together in bed, whispering and trying to be quiet. My mother would for sure have her ears perked. Tony would be watching through the keyhole and Lionel's mother would be listening against the other wall.

The sound stopped me still again. This time it didn't end immediately. It was a scratching noise, like a rat or some other small animal. Lionel wasn't outside. Maybe it wasn't a small animal. Maybe it was a leopard. My window was open. Jumping out of bed, I ran over and latched it shut. Lionel wasn't going to come. He'd be too modest, too worried about getting caught. He made me angry. We should have moved in together. There's nothing wrong with that as long as you get married in the end.

I imagined his parents staying on for weeks. I'd have to be a bride forever and never a wife. Maybe they'd keep us in separate rooms until they wanted grandchildren. They'd regulate us with special hours and ration our nights together. I put my nightgown on again and tried to fall asleep.

In the morning, as the sun hit the tops of the pine trees outside my window, a servant brought me a miniature pot of tea and a plate of scones. I felt better. The noise outside the window was gone. It must have been a rat or a shrew. The tea woke me up slowly, not with the abruptness of coffee. As I was pouring a second cup, Mrs Saunders shouted in to me that there was hot water in the bathroom when I wanted it. Bathing, dressing, combing my hair, I felt more relaxed and fresh. Debrakot seemed so different from the night before. I told myself that yesterday I'd just been tired and it had made me irritable.

Lionel took me to breakfast at his house and we sat alone at the table and giggled over porridge and eggs.

'Well, wife,' he said, imitating Mr Saunders' tone of voice, 'do you think you can stand looking at my mug every morning for the rest of your life?'

'The tiger showed me his tattoo last night.'

'Oh, did he? That was fresh of him.'

'Do they have any children?'

'One chap in England who married a striptease dancer.'
'And you were worried about us causing a scandal!'

Latif prepared a picnic lunch for us and we rode out to a hilltop about a mile from the house. There were two beautiful chestnut trees under which we spread a tablecloth. It was still early and we decided to take a walk. The horses grazed while we wandered down the ridge. No one was around. The mountains were folded and wrinkled like a pile of rumpled clothes. It seemed as if we were the only people anywhere.

The town inflicted a code of morals on Lionel and he always seemed to be worried about what other people might think. Alone with him it felt more like it did in Delhi, where he ignored who or what the two of us were and treated me the whole time as if I was the only other person in the world.

'Why do you let these people dictate to you?' I finally asked.

He laughed. 'I used to ignore them. To me they were just silly old Anglo-Indians nostalgic about a period which had passed.'

'And now you've changed your mind.'

'No, not exactly. What I realized was that they are our people, Sylvia, and we are all that will be left of them in a few years.'

'I don't want to be a relic.'

'That's not what I mean,' he said.

'You want to preserve all of their silliness?'

'No, it can't last. But there's no point in destroying it.'

'Even if it stands between the two of us?'

'All their lives they've been concerned with one thing, their legitimacy. Nobody allowed them that, neither the Indians nor the English.'

'You mean they're all orphans in a sense.'

Lionel twisted his head to one side cautiously. 'No, you can't say something as simple as that. It's just that we're part of their legitimacy. Something like a marriage is very important to them because it reaffirms their community. You're right, it's only the two of us getting married but on the other hand, since we're both part of their community, it's like putting another nail in the board or adding another stitch to the seam.'

We found a stand of young pine trees where the ground was soft and springy with their needles.

'You know, I was hoping you were going to come to my room last night,' I said.

I waited for him to say he had seen me in the window but he only raised his eyebrows.

'For what?' he asked, and then laughed.

We kissed slowly as if we were hunting for something. I opened my eyes and looked at him. His face seemed different so close to mine. I thought of the first time we made love, in my room in Delhi. I had only met him three days before but it seemed as if I had been waiting for years. I was a virgin, frightened but eager. After he undressed me I kept my legs together tightly for a long time. But the tighter I pressed them together, the more I wanted him to pry them open.

The mountains seemed so deserted that I decided no one would find us. Being naked in the middle of the day, in the middle of the forest, made me feel like some sort of animal. I wanted to run down the hill, taking long strides, leaping over bushes, logs, trees, from one mountain to the next.

We collided like clouds on a windy day. Wrapped around each other, tangled. He came over me like a shadow. I felt my body purse up. It was like touching a live wire. The electricity burned through me. I couldn't let go.

The sunny morning had made me feel so innocent and careless. My fears had dissipated and were spread out at a distance from me. Lionel seemed to draw everything together. It was like pulling an unravelling thread and having the cloth bunch up. He sucked my emotions far up inside himself. Then he shot them all back into me. It was a transfusion of everything I had felt in the last day and a half, all at once.

I cried without trying to stop myself. The tears flushed me but left me feeling abandoned. Lionel thought he had hurt me and gently brushed the pine needles out of my hair. His voice was low and caressing. The seconds eloped with each other. I pulled him back down against me and cried into his shoulder.

'Why can't we get married right now?' I said.

He didn't answer.

'Let's just ignore everyone. I won't sleep alone another night.'

He whispered my name a couple of times.

'But everything's arranged,' he said.

'I don't care. Those arrangements aren't for us. They're for our parents and everyone else. They don't mean anything to us.'

'But are you sure now?' he asked. 'What if I turn into a lame tiger and you become an ostrich?'

I couldn't laugh.

'I don't want you to do it for me. Can you stand living away from Delhi? Think of yourself, Sylvia.'

'Lionel, don't say that. Be selfish for once. Take me and keep me. I want to be with you from now on. I won't spend another night at the Saunderses' house.'

'Will you be happy here?'

'Yes.'

'Well, if you're sure, Padre Joseph has the licences all ready. It would take five minutes, if that's what you want.'

'You mean he could marry us today?' I asked, surprised.

'Sure. We can let him read a psalm and say a prayer if we want. His wife will witness it in their house.'

'What about the rest of the town?' I asked.

'Now look who's worried.'

'We won't tell anyone,' I said.

'No, we won't until afterwards.'

'But it will be *quite* legitimate.'

'Let them find out for themselves,' said Lionel. 'It will be a good surprise. Get dressed quickly.'

Padre Joseph was a portly south Indian Christian. He looked at us suspiciously when we told him what we wanted. Maybe he could tell that we had just come from making love. He took us into the sanctuary and opened a small drawer in the pulpit. Our marriage licences were signed. His wife came in looking uncertain and added her name to the certificate; they both looked baffled. Padre Joseph rambled out an irrelevant prayer in which he discussed politics with God but not our wedding. Lionel gave a hundred rupees to the church offering, which cheered him up.

We had forgotten our lunch at the picnic spot. Latif sent a boy to retrieve it and made us high tea. The evening glow was beginning to spread over the mountains. Lionel and I sat on the veranda. A few minutes before, we had seen a flustered Padre Joseph racing up the path to the Saunderses' house. The whole town would know soon enough. In the distance, on one of the ridges, there was a puff of dust. Another spurted up right next to it. A few seconds later the sound of the explosion reached us.

'They're blasting for the new road,' said Lionel.

'They're saluting us,' I said.

More About Penguins
and Pelicans

For further information about books available from Penguins please write to Dept EP, Penguin Books Ltd, Harmondsworth, Middlesex UB7 0DA.

In the U.S.A: For a complete list of books available from Penguins in the United States write to Dept CS, Penguin Books, 625 Madison Avenue, New York, New York 10022.

In Canada: For a complete list of books available from Penguins in Canada write to Penguin Books Canada Ltd, 2801 John Street, Markham, Ontario L3R 1B4.

In Australia: For a complete list of books available from Penguins in Australia write to the Marketing Department, Penguin Books Australia Ltd, P.O Box 257, Ringwood, Victoria 3134.

In New Zealand: For a complete list of books available from Penguins in New Zealand write to the Marketing Department, Penguin Books (N.Z.) Ltd, P.O. Box 4019, Auckland 10.

CLEAR LIGHT OF DAY

Anita Desai

'She *is* good' – Susan Hill

To the family living in the shabby, dusty house in Delhi, Tara's visit brought a sharp reminder of life outside the traditional pattern. For Bim, coping endlessly with their problems there is a renewal of the old jealousies, for she has failed to escape like her sister. But escape to what?

Anita Desai adroitly focuses on the tensions of life in a changing society. Her subtle and cleverly observed book skilfully pulls together past and present to reveal in small preoccupations and minute shifts of feeling a larger, bigger world.

A BACKWARD PLACE

Ruth Prawer Jhabvala

The trouble with Bal was not his lack of ideas but the fact that they tended to be rather grand long-term visions whereas his life was organized on a decidedly short-term basis. And for Judy his English wife, Etta the ageing sophisticate, Clarissa the upper middle-class drop-out from the English establishment, the worthy Hochstadts on a two-year exchange visit, and all the other characters who figure in this enchanting novel, India always poses a host of contradictions.

'One questions whether any western writer has had a keener, cooler understanding of the temperament of urban India' – *Guardian*

AN AREA OF DARKNESS

V. S. Naipaul

Coming from a family which left India only two generations ago, V. S. Naipaul felt that his roots lay in India. But the country and its attitudes remained outside his experience, in an 'area of darkness', until, with some apprehension, he spent a year there. He arrived at Bombay, then travelled as far north as Kashmire, east to Calcutta and south to Madras. Here he shares his experience of India generously and gives the reader deep insight into a country and a writer's mind.

'Tender, lyrical, explosive ... excellent' – John Wain

'Most compelling and vivid' – V. S. Pritchett

OLD SOLDIERS

Paul Bailey

In flight from painful memories, Victor Harker encounters the extraordinary Captain Hal Standish. Drawn together in an uneasy alliance, the two men find they have unexpected ghosts in common.

'I was deeply moved ... It is very witty on the surface, but underneath heartrendingly sad ... a beautiful example of his work' – C. P. Snow

'Spare, intense, eliptical ... *Old Soldiers* has taken root in my head' – *Sunday Times*

THE STORIES OF JOHN CHEEVER

'A very impressive display of Cheever's powers ... He lies, in American writing, somewhere between Scott Fitzgerald and John Updike ... These are stories of love and squalor, set in a world in which momentary glimpses of brightness – sea, clouds, light, the East River, a wife in a torn slip at the dressing table – contend with time, social change, and the chaos of history' – Malcolm Bradbury in the *New Statesman*

THE TRANSIT OF VENUS

Shirley Hazzard

Two sisters, Grace and Caro Bell, emigrate to England from Australia in the 1920s in search of their lives. Within the larger world of ideological clashes and social hunger, the sisters make their individual journeys towards middle age. For Caro, whose destiny is to love and be loved, the price includes betrayal. For Grace, who risks less, knowledge tempered with anguish comes too late.

'An extraordinary book' – *Sunday Times*

'Sumptuous ... impeccable' – *The Times*